He and Tito had found themselves in a stolen GTO being driven by Tito's dimwitted cousin Raoul, and when Raoul got too drunk to drive, Kennin had "disposed" of the vehicle.

Mercado pressed his fingers into a tent and looked thoughtful. "One thing about the casino business, Kennin. People are always looking for a connection between us and the bad guys. Granted, they have good reason. Up till recently the business was strictly mob run. But that's changed. The gaming commission smells any connection to the mob now and you can lose your casino license. That's serious stuff, understand?"

Kennin nodded slowly.

"Normally, I'd hear a story like that, and given what happened with you and my car the other day, that would be the end of you," Mercado went on. "But I also hear you're the most talented drifter around. If this drifting thing is gonna work, I'm gonna need you. But you gotta stay out of trouble, understand? 'Cause next time there ain't gonna be a next time."

battle drift

By Todd Strasser

ILLUSTRATED BY CRAIG PHILLIPS

Simon Pulse
New York London Toronto Sydney

SIMON PULSE
An imprint of Simon & Schuster Children's Publishing Division
1230 Avenue of the Americas, New York, NY 10020
Text copyright © 2006 by Todd Strasser
Illustrations copyright © 2006 by Craig Phillips
All rights reserved, including the right of reproduction in whole or in part in any form.
SIMON PULSE and colophon are registered trademarks of Simon & Schuster, Inc.
Designed by Sammy Yuen Jr.
The text of this book was set in Trade Gothic.
Manufactured in the United States of America
First Simon Pulse edition April 2006
10 9 8 7 6 5 4 3 2
Library of Congress Control Number 2005930631
ISBN-13: 978-1-4169-0582-0
ISBN-10: 1-4169-0582-0

This book is dedicated to
Ron "Get to the Ball Game on Time" Sher.

I would like to thank the following organization and people for their mostly helpful (and sometimes humorously wiseass) comments and assistance:

Amanda Sohr, Dan Carluch, DGTrials.com, Troy "Driftmonkey" Holloway, Chachi, Alex, Thoraxe, LookOutMatt, Gram, I Love Sweatpants, d4vech3n, EunosGangstarr, Darkbane, 1.8turbo510, Shiftnslide, Die Screaming, Airjockie, Dr. Baby, Drift Machine, Thon, Dragracingunderground, VQ Driver, ECDA, Knives, Kata, Toycoma, Mikespeed95, fraggleSTICKcar, Ichi-Go, Dominican Drift, Drew, Davis, Mistatwo, Thrwnsprkz, Moorefire, Saru of the West, Forsaken TH, Trunk, Dave Chen, Dori FC, Vosko, Mranlet.

battle drift

1

Kennin Burnett stood in front of the open garage door at Rivera's Service Center and gazed off toward the dull brown mountains in the distance. Dark mare's tails of rain hung down from the solid gray ceiling of clouds above. It was hard to tell whether the rain was hitting the ground or evaporating in the air. If it was hitting the ground, it meant trouble for the drift tsuiso that night. Drifting was all about pushing the edge of control to the limit. It was hard enough on dry roads. On wet roads that edge blurred into nothingness. A dark, sinister nothingness that Kennin had brushed up against once before with deadly results.

From inside the garage Angelita Rivera watched him. She was leaning against the blue Nissan 240 SX she'd built for drifting. Until a few days ago, she'd planned to sell this ride. It was the fourth car she'd modified and she felt like she was getting better and better at it. She knew she could sell it for good money. Money that would go toward the college education she could never otherwise afford.

But then her idiot brother, Tito, had messed up her plan. He'd bet every cent he had on Kennin winning the drift battle tonight. Only Kennin didn't have a car, so if Angelita didn't let him use the 240 SX, Tito would lose it all. She'd had no choice, right? She *had* to let Kennin use the car. It was the only way to save Tito's sorry butt.

Don't lie to yourself, Angelita thought. *That's not the real reason you're letting Kennin drive your car.* If Kennin hadn't been standing so close, she might have scolded herself out loud. Who did she think she was kidding? The real reason she was letting Kennin use the car had nothing to do with her brother. The real reason was that somehow this dark-haired, good-looking, mysterious boy had gotten past her defenses and undermined her plans. He was a thief who'd picked the lock that protected her heart.

And the saddest part was that he didn't even know it.

Kennin turned and gazed at her with those piercing dark eyes. "Know where Tito is?"

"You joking?" Angelita asked back. As if she'd have a clue what her flaky brother was up to.

Kennin strolled toward the 240 SX and placed his hand on the roof. The paint was sun dulled and faded. From a distance this ride looked like your basic clunker street vehicle. But close up was a different story. This was a true drift car. Angelita had gutted the interior and added the roll cage and racing bucket with four-point harness. Kennin had seen the SR20DET with a GT2871R turbo and supporting mods under the hood.

"Anyone drifted this beast yet?" he asked.

"Not since I got hold of it." Angelita felt a burst of pride at his obvious appreciation of her work.

"A virgin, huh?" Kennin said.

Not the only one in this garage, Angelita thought with unexpected yearning, then quickly caught herself. *Are you crazy, girl? What are you thinking? You've got plans. Next year you're out of here and going to college. He may be a dish, but there'll be no more of this nonsense.*

But even as those warnings crossed her mind, she felt a magnetic force drawing her closer to the car and the hot guy standing beside it.

"Know what I like?" Kennin asked, sliding his hand over the hood of the Nissan. "You didn't cover it with stupid stickers."

"You mean, you can't turn a vehicle into a drift car just by covering it with product logos?" Angelita joked.

They stood close to each other and shared a knowing smile. Agreeing silently that when it came to cars, a showy outside meant nothing. It was what was inside that counted. Standing side by side, looking at the car, their shoulders almost touched. Angelita could hear Kennin's steady breaths. If she'd turned her head and leaned toward him, she could have pressed her lips against his.

"Yo, wazup?" At the unexpected sound of Tito's voice they jumped and spun around. Angelita's brother stepped into the garage. He was a medium-size kid with curved shoulders from way too many hours spent hunched over controllers playing Need for Speed Underground and GT-4. The stoop of his shoulders made him look smaller than he really was.

Tito studied his sister and Kennin. "Hey, hope I wasn't interrupting anything."

From the grin on her brother's lips, Angelita could tell that he was joking. He had no idea how close she and Kennin might have come if he hadn't appeared.

"We've been waiting for you," she said.

"Yeah, sorry I'm late," Tito said. "You guys ready for the big tsuiso?"

Once again Kennin gazed out the garage doors at the ominous gray wisps hanging from the clouds in the distance. Under normal circumstances dark, wet mountain roads were just plain dangerous. Battle drifting on them was nothing short of suicidal. Once again, the painful memories threatened to overtake him. Kennin nodded. "Yeah, let's hit it."

They hesitated for a moment before getting into the car. Since Angelita was the only one with a driver's license, it made sense that she'd drive. Kennin and Tito glanced in through the windows. In the space where the rear seat had once been were spare tires, the jack, an electric impact wrench, and Kennin's black G-Force helmet. There was barely enough space left for one small person to squeeze into, and no way to sit comfortably. Standing outside the car, Tito and Kennin gave each other looks. Broad shouldered and nearly six feet tall, Kennin was four inches taller than Tito.

"Guess I'm riding in the back," Tito grumbled sourly and started to climb in. "Ah! Ooh! Ouch!" He made plenty of complaining noises as he squeezed himself into the back with the tires, jack, and other gear. Meanwhile, Kennin got in next to Angelita.

With a *whoosh* of the turbo, she started the car and pulled out of the garage and onto the street. Sitting next to her, Kennin could tell by how the car reacted that the steering was tight and the suspension well tuned. Despite his misgivings about running in the rain, he began to feel an eagerness to get behind the wheel and see what this beater could do.

"Sounds sweet," he said as Angelita increased throttle pressure and the car accelerated smoothly.

"Thanks," she said. She would have preferred a compliment about herself, but one about her car was almost as good. They went around a corner and she gave the accelerator an extra tap, just to show him how peppy the engine was.

From the back came a *clank!* Then a *clunk!* First Kennin's helmet, and then the jack, fell onto Tito.

"Hey!" Angelita's brother yelped as he pushed the jack off him. "Take it easy, okay?"

"Sorry," Angelita called back, glad her brother couldn't see the grin on her face. They got on Las Vegas Boulevard and headed out of town, passing a seemingly endless number of strip malls, wedding chapels, and every imaginable kind of fast-food restaurant.

Kennin felt a tap on his shoulder from behind. "So, *mi amigo,* psyched about tonight?" Tito asked.

Kennin glanced at the heavy gray clouds in the distance and shrugged.

"Come on, dude, you should be pumped," Tito urged him. "This is your chance to show the world what you got. And don't forget that I got every freakin' penny I own riding on you. I mean, dude, seriously, if I was in your shoes I'd be flipping."

"We've noticed," Angelita deadpanned.

"Huh?" Tito realized she was teasing him. "Hey, screw you. Just 'cause I don't have ice water running through my veins like you guys . . ."

Kennin pointed through the windshield. "I'd be more psyched if I knew for sure that rain wasn't hitting the ground."

"Rain?" Tito craned his neck around the spare tires and stared out the side window. "*Carajo!* You think they'll run if the roads are wet?"

"Only one way to find out," Kennin answered.

After that, Tito, who was usually a motormouth when he was nervous or excited, was actually silent for a while. Angelita drove east. They were on the incline into the foothills when the first tiny drops of mist began to collect on the windshield. Not enough to turn on the wipers, but still a bad omen.

In the back, Tito broke his silence. "So, uh, Kennin, you ever drift in the rain before?"

Kennin winced. The question brought forth the very memories he'd been running from ever since he left Pasadena. He slouched down in his seat and pressed his fingertips together. The skin beside his eyes wrinkled. Next to him, Angelita was puzzled. It didn't seem like such a big deal, and yet Kennin reacted as if he'd just been asked a deeply personal, painful question.

"Kennin?" Tito said after a moment.

"Sorry," Kennin said as if coming out of a daydream. "Uh, yeah, I've run in the rain."

"How is it?" Tito asked.

"Slippery."

"But you can do it, right?" Tito asked anxiously.

Kennin didn't want Tito to worry. Then again, he hadn't wanted him to make all those bets, either. Things would have been a lot easier if he hadn't. Kennin could have turned down the challenge to battle drift and gone on with his life.

Angelita knew that drifting in the rain was incredibly

risky. And on wet mountain roads it could be lethal to both cars and drivers. Angelita wasn't worried that much about the car being wrecked. It could be fixed. Or, at the worst, junked. Wrecked human bodies were a different story.

A lot harder to fix.

And junking wasn't an option.

She stared at the moisture on the windshield as it gradually collected into larger drops that ran sideways off the glass. Finally she turned to Kennin and said, "You don't have to do this, you know."

Kennin slowly nodded. He knew.

2

They drove up into the foothills. Dark curtains of droplets fell in the distance, and the clouds overhead were a solid ceiling of gray. The mist was getting thicker, and the road surface was darkening with moisture.

"Could you pull over?" Kennin asked Angelita.

"Something wrong?" Tito blurted nervously from the back.

"Just feel bad about you being cramped in the back like that," Kennin said while Angelita pulled the car over onto the gravel shoulder.

"Serious?" Tito asked.

"Why don't you sit in the front?" Kennin said, climbing out of the car and feeling the cool moisture on his face.

"What about you?" Tito asked, getting out.

"I'll get in the back," Kennin said.

"Why?"

"He wants to study the course," Angelita said from inside the car.

Smart girl, thought Kennin as he squeezed into the back beside the spare tires, his nose close enough to smell the rubber. What had been a tight fit for Tito felt like a sardine can for him. He managed to wedge himself in and watched out the back window, studying each turn, trying to imagine how it would appear when he was drifting back down.

They reached the top of the mountain and pulled into the scenic overlook. The mist spread a dull finish over everything it touched. Half a dozen cars were already there, including *Slide or Die*, Chris Craven's metallic red, ultra-tweaked 240 SX. As usual at any gathering of drifters, hoods were open and guys were crowding around, checking out the latest mods. Cigarette smoke was in the air and the sounds of loud music and ratcheting impact wrenches hammered their ears.

"Looks like the gang's all here," Tito said, and started to push open his door. Still squeezed into the back, Kennin didn't move.

"You coming?" Tito asked him.

"In a minute," Kennin said. "You guys go ahead."

Tito and Angelita got out and stood in the mist. The gray daylight was gradually fading. Somewhere behind the dark clouds the sun had begun to set. A revving engine caught their attention. The next car to pull into the overlook was a white Toyota Cressida with black spoke rims. Neither Tito nor Angelita had seen it before.

"Danger gremlin?" Tito guessed.

Angelita shook her head. "He's here to drift."

"Thing looks stock," said Tito.

His sister pointed at the tires. "Eighteen-inch-high performance rubber. And see through the spokes? Cross-drilled custom discs."

Tito squinted at the bright red disc brakes visible through the rims. Of course his sister was right. He should have known better than to doubt her when it came to cars.

The Cressida's door opened and the stocky redheaded football player thug named Ian got out. As usual he was wearing a baseball cap backward. His gaze immediately met Tito's. Ian smirked. "Where's slanty-eyes?"

Neither Angelita nor Tito answered. Ian was always taunting them and looking for a fight. Getting no rise out of Angelita or her brother, he joined his friends in the crowd.

A moment later Angelita and Tito were joined by Kennin, who'd finally gotten out of the car. "What was that about?" he asked.

Tito and his sister shared a look. "Nothing," Angelita said.

"Ian was just being a jerk, as usual," added Tito. "Frickin' racist. Come on, we better get the comp tires on."

While Kennin jacked up the rear end, Tito got out the electric impact wrench and began to undo the lug nuts. The ratcheting sound filled the air. The mist covered everything, making metal slippery and clothing damp.

More cars arrived. Some belonged to competitors, others to friends or posers. A light blue Toyota Corolla with metallic silver racing stripes pulled up, and Mutt got out wearing his black and red racing jacket. Mutt was one half of the team of Mutt and Megs, the self-appointed starters and tsuiso coordinators. A chubby guy with short brown hair and a bad case of zits, Mutt could always be found at drifting events with a cell phone in one hand and dull green megaphone in the other. He waved at Kennin. "You really want to run in this soup?"

"Just give me the word," Kennin answered.

The next car to arrive was Driftdog Dave's 180 SX hatchback, the red paint still scorched black from the fire a few weeks before when it had blown its engine and started to burn.

Tito looked up from the wheel he was tightening. "Hey, look who got his ride going."

The hatchback stopped and the window came down. From the driver's seat Driftdog reached out and grabbed Kennin's hand. He had long brown hair pulled back into a ponytail and a scar through his left eyebrow. "What's shakin'? How's the arm?"

The night of the fire, Kennin had burned his arm pulling Driftdog out of the flaming car just moments before guys with extinguishers arrived to put out the blaze.

"Better, thanks." Kennin patted the hatchback's roof. "How'd you get this thing running?"

"Lucked into a CA18DET in a junkyard," Driftdog said. "Couldn't frickin' believe it. Can't say I've got her running at optimum power yet, but at least I'm here. That's what counts, right?"

"Right," Kennin answered.

Driftdog rubbed his fingers along the edge of the moisture-speckled windshield. "So what do you think?"

"It is what it is," Kennin replied.

"Yeah," agreed Driftdog, "and what it is sucks. But what can you do, right?"

"Run unless they tell us not to," Kennin said.

"Well, good luck, pal. Tonight we'll need it." Driftdog put the 180 SX hatchback into gear, revved the engine, and continued up the road. Kennin strolled back to Angelita and Tito. Waves of mist drifted across the dark mountaintop. Each time a car came up the mountain road, a billion tiny drops of water sparkled in its headlights.

Tito finished getting the comp tires on and jacked the car down.

"We live in the frickin' desert," he muttered as he pulled the jack away and wiped the moisture off his forehead. "Two hundred and fifty days of sunshine a year and tonight we have to get this."

From the looks on the faces of the others around the overlook, it was obvious that Tito was not the only one feeling that way. Eyes were turned upward toward the dark clouds. Drivers frowned and shook their heads, clearly annoyed and disappointed. Suddenly all the grumbling stopped and heads turned as a bright red Lexus IS300 pulled in.

"Sweet ride!" Tito groaned with admiration.

They couldn't see the driver through the dark windows, but next to Chris Craven's 240 SX, this had to be the hottest car in the overlook. And, by a long shot, the most expensive.

"Who do we know who could afford those kind of wheels?" Tito wondered aloud.

He didn't have to wait long for the answer. The IS300's door opened, and Mariel Lewis, the sexiest girl in school, got out.

3

Angelita paid close attention to what happened next. Mariel crossed her arms, leaned against her Lexus, and shot a look at her boyfriend, Chris Craven, who was standing a dozen yards away talking with a group of guys. It was obvious that she wanted him to come over and say hello. But Chris merely glanced in her direction and then turned back to his friends. Almost as if he didn't recognize her.

Mariel's eyes narrowed and her mouth grew tight. She gazed around the overlook and stopped when she saw Kennin. Her eyes relaxed and returned to their normal size, while a smile appeared on her lips. Angelita could almost see the devious plan hatching in that hussy's mind.

Just then Mutt pressed the megaphone to his lips and announced, "All drivers over here."

Slowly the drivers, and some of their friends, strolled over. Kennin went with Tito and Angelita. Their path crossed right in front of Ian and his football player friends.

"Look, it's the boat people," Ian cracked. "So where's your hired assassin and his butterfly knife?"

He was talking about an incident a few weeks before at a pool party at Mariel's house. Ian had taunted Kennin about being half Asian. Just before it turned into an all-out brawl, Tito's cousin Raoul had pulled out a butterfly knife, which instantly calmed everyone down.

Now at the overlook, Tito turned to Ian. "What are you trying to do?"

"Ain't it obvious?" Ian said. "I'm telling you you're not wanted here."

"That's weird. I seem to recall that Chris went out of his way to make sure my friend ran in this tsuiso," Tito said, and gestured to Kennin.

"Hey, everybody makes mistakes," Ian shot back.

"Far as I can tell, the only person who doesn't want us here is you," Angelita said to him. "So why don't you keep it to yourself, okay?"

Before Ian could come up with some new wiseass answer, Mutt broke in.

"Take it somewhere else, okay? That ain't what we're here for." He turned to the crowd. "Okay, guys, I guess there's one question on everyone's mind. We gonna run tonight or not?"

"What's the problem?" someone asked. "Slick roads'll just make it easier to drift."

"Easier to lose control, numb nuts," muttered someone else.

"I'll tell you one thing we won't have to worry about," said Ian. "The cops. They'll never expect drifting on a night like tonight."

"For good reason," said Driftdog Dave.

The crowd appeared divided. Because Chris was considered the best driver and was kind of a leader anyway, people tended to look in his direction when big decisions needed to be made. Meanwhile, Mariel, wearing a gray hoodie to protect her blond hair from the moisture, edged her way through the crowd and squeezed between Angelita and Kennin.

Angelita shot her a dirty look but knew better than to make a scene, which she knew was exactly what Mariel wanted. Instead, she shrugged and stepped aside as if she couldn't care less.

"What do you think, Chris?" Mutt asked.

Chris looked at Kennin and Mariel and frowned. He caught Kennin's eye for an instant, then looked away. But in that instant, Kennin saw a glimmer of doubt. Wet roads weren't something drivers around Las Vegas had a lot of experience with. Drifting might be the art of driving without traction, but it was crucial for every driver to feel the fine line where traction ended and drifting began. Kennin knew only too well how that line could become blurred on steep mountain roads.

Kennin felt a hand on his arm and stiffened, thinking it was Mariel. He felt someone's warm breath close to his ear and relaxed. Without turning around, he knew it was Angelita from the scent of her perfume. She must have circled around behind him and was now standing on his left. "Like I said, you don't have to run tonight," she whispered.

Kennin turned his head toward her. "I won't if you don't want me to. It's your car."

"It's not the car I'm worried about," Angelita whispered back.

"Aw, isn't that cute," Mariel smirked from Kennin's right.

"Mind your own business," Angelita said.

"Chris wouldn't be afraid to run," Mariel said just loudly enough for her boyfriend and the other drivers to hear. Chris had been looking up at the dark, wet sky, but now his gaze returned to Mariel.

"What do you want to do?" Mutt asked him.

By now, almost every trace of daylight was gone. Running in the dark was always more difficult than running in daylight. It was harder to gauge distances and judge turns. And that was before you factored in the wet roads. Kennin imagined Chris was feeling the mist on his face. He wiped the moisture off his helmet.

"I say we give it a shot," Chris finally said.

To Kennin the decision was no surprise. Not when

Mariel was around to mock anyone who might have the sense to say no. From the discontented muttering that followed, Kennin definitely had the feeling that the other drivers would have preferred not running tonight. Mutt passed around a hat with numbered index cards in it. "Everyone take one."

Kennin reached in and pulled out a card with "#7" scrawled on it.

"Hey, Chris," said Driftdog. "What do you say everyone gets a couple of practice runs? So at least we'll know what we're dealing with."

"We start doing practice runs and we'll be here half the frickin' night," Chris said. "We've all run this course before. I say we run the tsuiso just like any other time."

That ended the discussion. Everyone headed back to their cars. Walking beside Kennin, Tito clapped his hands together eagerly. "Yeah, let's get this show on the road!"

Kennin couldn't blame him. The kid was eager to get his money back.

They ran into Driftdog. The mist had matted his long brown hair against his head. "Guess we're gonna go, huh?" He didn't sound thrilled.

"Looks like it," said Kennin.

"I'd be happier in pouring rain than this stuff," Driftdog muttered.

"You serious?" asked Tito.

"Damn straight. Oil's lighter than water," Driftdog said. "You get a light rain or mist like this, the water just brings all the oil on the road up to the surface. It gets real slick and spotty. At least when it rains hard the oils get washed away and the road surface is pretty consistent."

"How do you know that hasn't already happened?" Tito asked. "Maybe the road's already wet enough."

"The trouble is, no one really knows," said Angelita.

"Man, I just don't want to be in the first heat," Driftdog said. "At least if you run later maybe one of your friends'll call and tell you what to watch out for. But the first guys down are the ones who'll really have to figure it out on their own."

They got to Driftdog's red 180 SX hatchback and stopped.

"Well, good luck, dude," Driftdog said to Kennin. "Guess we're lucky these mountain roads have guardrails." He made a fist, and Kennin tapped the knuckles with a fist of his own.

A few cars down, Kennin, Tito, and Angelita stopped beside the blue 240 SX. In the dark the car looked black. The mist had started to collect in drops that ran down the windows and frame.

"Better put the street tires back on," Angelita said.

"No way," Tito groaned. "I just took 'em off."

"Think I'll need the extra traction?" Kennin asked.

Angelita nodded.

"Well, great," Tito grumbled, picking up the impact wrench. "What are you waiting for? Someone jack up the car so I can take off all the tires I just put on."

Kennin jacked up the car and Tito went to work. Over the music and sounds of impact wrenches came a loud argument. Mariel was making a scene, her hands on her hips, snapping at Chris, "I am really sick of your attitude!"

The guys hovering around *Slide or Die* stared at her nervously, but Chris merely turned his back, snubbing her.

"You are going to be so sorry!" Mariel shouted, and then stormed away. Angelita tensed, knowing precisely what would happen next. Mariel was heading straight for Kennin, and it was obvious she wanted to make sure Chris saw what was happening too.

"Is this yours?" Mariel asked loudly and gestured at the blue 240 SX.

"No, it's hers." Kennin gestured to Angelita.

"Really?" Mariel cocked her head. "My, we do have inventive ways of getting guys, don't we?"

Angelita ignored her.

"I hope she didn't just come right out and give you this car," Mariel said loudly. "I mean, that would really be the height of desperation."

"She's letting me use it tonight," Kennin replied calmly. "I guess you could say I'm test-driving it for her."

"Oh?" Mariel said. "I wonder what else she lets you do for her."

Angelita could feel her blood start to boil. She knew Mariel was trying to pick a fight, get Chris's attention, and stir things up. She also knew that the worst thing she could do was get into a catfight. But sometimes emotions overpowered logic.

"Back off, Mariel," Angelita warned. "We all know you're only doing this because your boyfriend's ignoring you and you want attention, okay? But we're really trying to get ready for the tsuiso tonight, and it would be a lot easier if you'd just get lost."

Of course this was just the response Mariel had been hoping for. Raising her voice, she yelled, "Who do you think you are, you little tramp?"

"You're calling me a tramp?" Angelita exploded. "You strut around school dressed like a hooker trying to tempt every guy you see to climb into your shorts, and you have the nerve to call *me* a tramp?"

Given the choice between breaking up a fight between guys or girls, Kennin would always choose guys. With girls, you really had to watch out for the nails. He managed to get in between them. But keeping the two clawing girls apart wasn't easy. Tito grabbed Angelita by the arm and started to yank. Mutt rushed over and helped pull her away. Meanwhile, Kennin put his arms around Mariel's waist and pulled her in the opposite direction.

"What the hell?" It was Chris, no doubt annoyed to find Kennin with his arms around Mariel's waist. Mariel didn't help matters when she instantly went from alley cat to purring feline, twisting around to face Kennin and caressing his dark hair as if they were in an embrace.

Kennin felt her press against him, felt her firm breasts bunch against his chest. His nostrils filled with the scent of her perfume. She was undeniably attractive, sensual, and desirable. It had been a long time since he'd been this close to someone so alluring.

"What do you think you're doing?" Chris marched up. Kennin tried to back away from Mariel, but she locked her arms around his waist.

"He's just being nice," Mariel shot back. "And paying a lot more attention to me than anyone else I know."

Just as Kennin managed to release himself from Mariel's grip, Ian joined the fracas. "Dude, you gonna let some gook put the moves on your girl?" he asked Chris.

There wasn't much that could set Kennin off when he was trying to get focused for a tsuiso. But one thing that was guaranteed to blow his gaskets was the kind of racist remarks Ian specialized in. With the blood in his veins pumping like a geyser, so hard he could feel the pulse in his forehead, Kennin spun around and waved Ian forward. "You're on, dillweed."

"Say what?" Ian came toward him. "You ready to get your butt whipped, China boy? Bring it on."

Kennin balled his hands into fists.

"Enough!" Carrying a tire iron, Driftdog Dave stepped into the middle of the crowd. "You guys wanna take this soap opera someplace else, be my guest. But right now we're here to drive, not mix it up with chicks and racists."

Kennin felt hands on his arms as Angelita and Tito pulled him away.

"Listen to Driftdog, dude," Tito said. "You gotta focus on driving tonight. Everything else can wait till tomorrow."

Kennin allowed himself to be led away. Tito was right. He had to think about the job at hand. His friend Doug had died drifting in the rain. Did he want the same thing to happen to him?

"Chicken," Ian called after him. "Pure chicken."

Kennin felt Tito's grip on his arms tighten. "Don't let him get to you. The guy's a frickin' retard. You want to beat him to a pulp tomorrow, be my guest. But tonight it's about the tsuiso and nothing else. *Comprendo, mi amigo?*"

They got back to Angelita's 240 SX. Needing a way to calm himself down, Kennin used a rag to wipe the film of mist off the side and rear windows. Tito sat in the car to get out of the damp, but Angelita stood outside with Kennin, the mist collecting in her dark hair, slowly matting it down.

"Maybe we should just forget it for tonight," she said once again. "It doesn't feel right. The vibe's all wrong."

"Your brother will be out a lot of money," Kennin replied.

"That's his problem, not yours," Angelita said. "It's bad enough that you want to drift on these mountain roads in the rain, but what's the point of running against these jerks?"

Kennin looked at her and felt an ironic smile on his lips. "It's funny, but to me, that's the *whole* point of doing it."

"You have nothing to prove to them," Angelita insisted.

"Maybe not," Kennin said. "But if they drive, I drive."

They were interrupted by Mutt on the megaphone. "Listen up, guys. We pulled the cards out of the hat. In the first heat it'll be number three against number seven."

Tito gave Kennin a droll look. "You're number seven, right?"

Kennin nodded. But he was hardly paying attention. Ian was coming toward him through the crowd again. It looked like the idiot just didn't know when to quit.

4

This time it was different. Kennin knew from experience that when you fought, you didn't watch your opponent's eyes, you watched his hands. Ian had one hand in his jacket pocket. Kennin tensed as the possibilities went though his head. Was it a knife? A gun? Was the guy that crazy?

"What the hell?" Tito gasped as he saw Ian coming with his hand in his pocket.

Ian whipped his hand out.

Kennin jumped back.

In Ian's hand was an index card with "#3" on it. On his face was a big, taunting grin.

"Jackass," Tito muttered.

Kennin relaxed, but his heart was still racing.

Ian winked. "See you at the starting line, *chico*." He turned and headed back toward his car.

It took Kennin a moment to catch his breath. He felt Tito pat him on the shoulder.

"Un-frickin'-believable." Tito chuckled with relief. "Congrats, dude. Looks like you and Ian get to be the guinea pigs."

Kennin got into Angelita's 240 SX. The mist was getting heavier and thicker. As he rolled the car up to the starting line, he had to turn on the windshield wipers. The moist air drifted in through the open window and collected on his helmet visor. Once again Kennin thought about Doug. It had been a night like this, but not even a serious competition. They'd just been out fooling around in a boosted car, too young and dumb to have any idea what they were doing. Just trying to get the feel of what it was like to hold a drifting car through a corner. Not even experienced enough to understand what it meant to be on rain-slicked pavement. Kennin had been behind the wheel and made just the tiniest of mistakes, and the next thing he knew the car was fishtailing, screeching, spinning. Then the ripping sound of rubber as it slid off the road shoulder, the loud crash as it went through the guardrail. Then the roller-coaster sensation of plummeting, the thunderous banging of sheet metal, the car rolling over and over, glass shattering, chunks of bumper flying. When the car stopped rolling, Kennin had found himself hanging upside down by the seat belt. Doug was no longer in the car.

Angelita leaned into the window of the 240 SX. "Hey."

Kennin was startled.

"Running the course in your head?"

"Uh, yeah." Kennin nodded, glad she couldn't get a good look at his eyes through the visor. If she had, she would have known he was lying.

"Have fun," she said. "Just don't get hurt."

"That's not very optimistic," Kennin said.

"It's realistic," said Angelita. She leaned in and kissed the side of his helmet.

Ian's white Toyota Cressida rolled up next to him. Inside, Ian tried to give him a tough look, but Kennin knew that if the guy had an ounce of brains in his head he would have been nervous as hell.

In the misty dark, Mutt stepped between the two cars and raised his right hand. His left hand pressed a cell phone to his ear as he spoke with Megs down the mountain at the finish line, making certain that the course was clear.

The tiny drops of mist were growing in size and becoming small drops of rain. Sitting in the 240 SX, Kennin watched the windshield wipers swipe back and forth. Deep inside he knew this was ridiculous. You couldn't seriously drift on roads as wet as these. The water blurred any ability to sense traction. But he was in this thing now and there was no backing away. He glanced through the water-streaked side window at the crowd. The rain was making some of the gawkers pack up and leave. Those who stayed were pulling the hoods of their sweatshirts up over their heads and jamming their hands into pockets. Those without hoods or hats had matted wet hair clinging to their heads or falling into their eyes.

Kennin heard a squeak and saw a hand wipe the rain off the passenger-side window. Angelita and Tito bent down and looked at him. Tito gave him a thumbs-up. Angelita pursed her lips and looked concerned.

Kennin winked at her.

"On your mark!" Mutt shouted with his arm still in the air. "Get ready! Get set!"

A moment of silence followed, and then Mutt brought his hand down.

Ian popped the clutch on the Cressida. That act alone showed Kennin how little the guy knew. The last thing you wanted to do on a night like tonight was jump out to the lead. The chasing driver would control the tsuiso. Not only that, but on the wet asphalt the only thing Ian managed to do was spin his wheels wildly. Kennin eased his clutch out slowly, feeling for the bite of the tires on the wet road surface. The heat had begun, but not the way he wanted it to.

Angelita had built a hot ride. The 240 SX had power to spare and was way too peppy for the current conditions. Kennin hardly drifted into the first turn while he waited for Ian to get control of the Cressida and catch up. As he came out of the turn he watched in the rearview mirror as Ian raced up behind him far too fast for the slippery conditions.

Kennin gritted his teeth, expecting that the guy would either rear-end him or lose it in the curve. The Cressida fish-tailed wildly, and Ian barely managed to get through the turn. Just as Kennin had suspected, the guy was proving to be a lightweight.

Kennin went into the next corner at half the speed he would have had the road been dry. He could have taken the turn considerably faster, but that wasn't the point. He wanted to see what Ian was capable of. And right now Ian was on his tail, which was the last place Kennin wanted him to be.

As they went into the next corner, Kennin purposefully got sideways too early and drifted wide. On the wet road surface, the tires made a squishy tearing-wet-cardboard sound. Like an amateur, Ian saw the opportunity, but hesitated. The cars came out of the turn the same as they'd gone in—with Kennin in the lead. He was starting to wonder if he'd have to actually pull over and park in order to give Ian the opportunity to go ahead.

They went into the next turn, and once again Kennin drifted the 240 SX early and wide. This time Ian took the bait. Cutting in tight, he passed Kennin on the inside. Now the Cressida was in front, where Kennin wanted him.

Had this been a serious tsuiso on dry roads, Kennin would have left Ian in the dust from the get-go. Or, had Ian been more of a contender, Kennin would have gotten on his tail and pushed him harder and harder until the guy lost

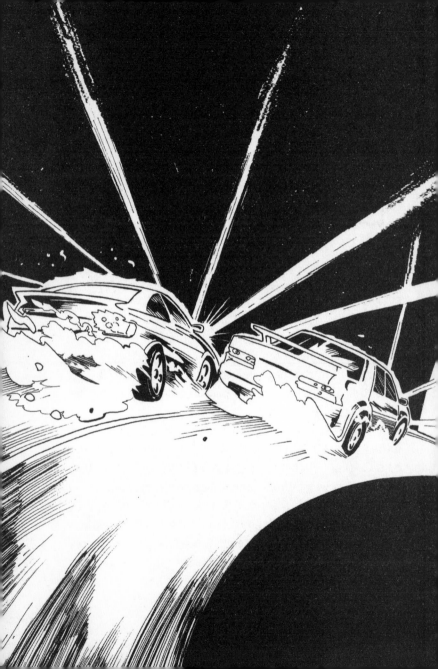

either his nerve or control of his car. But given the conditions and Ian's total lack of skill, it simply wasn't worth it. Instead, for the rest of the run, Kennin stayed on Ian's tail, nudging him slightly here and there as if he were trying to regain the lead, but never stalking the kid hard enough to really risk pushing him out of control.

As they went into the final S-turns at the bottom of the run, Kennin swung wide while Ian went in tight, trying to protect his lead. It was a typical beginner's mistake. Ian left the outside of the turn open and Kennin easily filled the vacancy. When they came out of the first S they were side by side, only now Kennin was on the inside position for the second turn. He drifted through it flawlessly, keeping the 240 SX sideways as long as he could to make sure Ian didn't have an opening to sneak through.

From there it was a short straight to the finish line, which Kennin crossed, two car lengths ahead of the white Cressida.

Hardly anyone was watching at the finish line. By now it was raining hard, and almost everyone at the bottom of the mountain had left. The few who remained sat in their cars. Kennin spotted Megs, the thin blond-haired half of the Mutt and Megs team, sitting in a red pickup, talking on a cell phone.

For Kennin, a tsuiso always ended with an odd emptiness. No checkered flag and no fans to cheer or congratulate you. Your friends were usually back up the mountain at the starting line. At the finish line it was just you and the other driver. If he was a good guy, you might get a begrudging compliment on your driving. But Kennin knew not to expect anything like that from Ian.

Kennin pulled off to the left side of the road. Ian pulled off to the right. Kennin killed the engine and listened to the metallic *pang-pang-pang* of the rain pelting the roof. For a moment he just sat in the 240 SX, his hands on the wheel, imagining what it would be like to run this car full out on dry pavement. It was definitely something he was looking forward to.

Bang! A car door slammed. Kennin jerked his head up and saw Ian storm through the rain toward him. *Now what?* Kennin wondered. He wasn't sure what Ian could be mad about, but the kid was unpredictable. Kennin had to make sure that whatever his problem was, he didn't take it out on Angelita's car.

Kennin got out and stood in the rain between Ian and the 240 SX.

"What the hell was that?" Ian pulled off his helmet and screamed at him.

Kennin didn't answer. He had no idea what the kid was ranting about.

"What? All of a sudden you don't know English?" Ian yelled. But he stopped on the wet asphalt half a dozen feet away, as if he was afraid to get too close.

Kennin removed his helmet and tucked it under his

arm. He felt the rain start to pelt his forehead and run down his face. "What's your problem?"

"My problem?" Ian repeated and pointed back up the mountain. "What was that? You think I don't know you let me pass you at the top? And then you just sat on my tail and waited? You didn't even drift through half those corners. That was no tsuiso. You didn't do anything until that last S-turn. And then you just snuck through."

"I don't remember any rules about how we're supposed to run a heat," Kennin said. "I can drive any way I want."

"They call it drifting for a reason, dillweed," Ian shot back. "You don't break traction, what's the point?"

Kennin was tempted to reply that driving against a punk newbie like Ian, there was no reason to break traction, but he didn't. Their argument was interrupted by the distant whine of engines up on the mountain as the next heat began. Ian and Kennin both looked up into the rainy dark. They could see the long shafts of headlights sweeping left and right through the mist and rain. Kennin walked over to the red pickup. Megs rolled down the window.

"Hey, congrats on your win," Megs said.

"Thanks," said Kennin, and pointed at the mountain. "Who's coming down?"

"Chris and Driftdog."

As if they'd temporarily forgotten their argument, both Kennin and Ian stared up at the mountain. From the high-pitched whines of the engines and the rubbery screeches, Kennin could tell that Chris and Driftdog were running harder than he and Ian had. And that meant they were taking more chances.

The beams of the headlights swung wildly in the dark rain and mist, and the tires made wet squealing sounds. Suddenly there was a high-pitched, loud screech that went on too long.

Clang! A loud metallic crash echoed through the damp air.

Now there was the sound of only one engine. Kennin could tell by the turbo gasp that it was Chris's 240 SX.

That meant that Driftdog had cracked up.

Chris's car cut out. Kennin imagined that he'd pulled off the road to check on Driftdog. Megs got out of the pickup and stood in the rain. "Was it Driftdog?"

Kennin nodded and felt rainwater soak his hair and seep down under his collar. Now he, Megs, and Ian stood in silence in the dark and waited. After a minute Megs's cell phone rang and he pressed it to his ear, hardly saying a word until, "Yeah, okay, gotcha."

Megs snapped the cell phone closed. "Driftdog's okay. He put the front end into the guardrail. But that's it, guys. We're calling it off. No one wants to risk getting their car smashed up."

Megs headed back toward the pickup. In the heavy rain, Ian turned to Kennin. "As far as I'm concerned, what happened tonight don't count. I'm looking forward to runnin' against you again. Only next time I'm gonna run your sorry butt right off the road."

Ian got back into the white Cressida. The lights went on, the wipers started to swish back and forth, and the engine roared to life. Kennin stood in the rain and watched as the car headed back toward Las Vegas. The guy had no clue how generous Kennin had been to him tonight. Driftdog had been unlucky, putting his front end in the guardrail. If Kennin had wanted to, he could have made sure Ian ended up there too. Next time he wouldn't be so nice.

5

Now that the tsuiso had been called off, there was no point in going back up the mountain. Borrowing Megs's cell phone, Kennin called Tito and Angelita and told them to get a ride down with the extra tires and gear. Then he got back into the car and waited. Looking up through the dark, misty rain he saw a caravan of headlights begin snaking down the side of the mountain. A little while later the first car reached the bottom. It was Mariel's bright red Lexus IS300. She pulled up beside the 240 SX and lowered her window. Kennin lowered his.

"I hear you won," she said.

"Driftdog okay?" Kennin asked.

Mariel nodded. "I passed him on the way down. His car's messed up, but he didn't have a scratch."

"Good."

Mariel bit her lips. "Look, about what happened before.

I don't want you to think I was using you to try and get Chris mad."

"What else am I supposed to think?" Kennin asked.

Mariel smiled, then purred, "Use your imagination, *papi*."

By now the next set of headlights had come down the mountain. It looked like a van.

"I like you, *papi*," Mariel said. "I bet you know how to treat a girl nice. And believe me, I know how to make you happy."

When the van pulled up behind the 240 SX and stopped, it caught both Kennin and Mariel by surprise. Kennin realized that whoever was driving must have given Angelita and Tito a ride down.

Angelita was the first to climb out of the van. She knew she shouldn't have been surprised to find Mariel's Lexus parked next to Kennin, but she was. Even in the dark, Angelita recognized the startled expression on Mariel's face. Like a little kid getting caught with her hand in the cookie jar. But for Angelita, it was also a glimpse of the truth. Up to now she'd assumed Mariel was simply using Kennin to make Chris jealous. But maybe it went deeper than that. Maybe trying to make Chris jealous was just a cover while she tested the waters with Kennin. That way, if Kennin blew her off, she could always claim she was just using him. The realization hit Angelita with a jolt. Mariel Lewis almost always got what she wanted. And if she was *that* hot for Kennin, then Angelita had some serious thinking to do.

Meanwhile, in the Lexus, Mariel gave Kennin a knowing look. "Think about what I said, okay, *papi*? I promise you won't be disappointed."

The Lexus pulled away just as Tito and Angelita got to the 240 SX. It was raining hard now, and Kennin could see that they were both soaked. He got out of the Nissan. "Angelita, you wait in the car. Come on, Tito, let's get the stuff out of the back of the van."

Like a typical brother, Tito complained, "How come she gets to sit in the car?"

"Because she's a girl, tough guy," Kennin said. As the rain poured down, he pulled open the van's rear door and yanked out the spare tires and the jack.

They got everything into the Nissan and climbed back in. Tito squeezed into the back and Kennin sat next to Angelita. The three of them were soaked to the skin. The car smelled like wet leather, and Kennin could hear Angelita's teeth chattering. Luckily the antifreeze in the cooling system was still hot, and they quickly got the heat going for the drive home.

"I heard Driftdog is okay," Kennin said.

"We passed him about halfway down the mountain," Tito said. "His whole left front end is smashed into the guardrail. That guy has the worst luck."

"Or he's lucky it wasn't worse," Kennin said.

"So, uh, what happened in your heat with Ian?" Tito asked.

"I won by a couple of lengths," Kennin said.

"Yeah, we heard about that," Tito said. "But what happened?"

"What do you mean?" Kennin asked, although he had a feeling he already knew what Tito meant.

"Well, no offense or anything, *mi amigo,* but Ian called his friends and said you drove like a real lardass."

Kennin smiled to himself. "You gotta be careful on wet roads."

"He said going into the first couple of corners you went wide on purpose to let him take the lead and then just followed him down the mountain like a frickin' Sunday driver."

"What's your problem, Tito?" Angelita asked. "He won, didn't he?"

"Just trying to get the feel of the road surface, you know?" Kennin added.

"You must've gotten it toward the bottom, because I heard that move you popped in the S-turns was pretty slick," Tito said.

Kennin shrugged. "Guess I got lucky."

"Yeah, guess you did," Tito echoed dubiously in a way that let Kennin know he didn't believe it. "Look, dude, I'm not trying to be critical or nothing, but I've got every cent I own riding on this. Maybe you can beat Ian that way, but you're never gonna beat Chris like that."

"Thanks for the advice," Kennin said.

"I am serious," Tito said. "I lose all my money, by the time I earn enough to get my own car I'll probably be too old to drive it."

"I'll try not to let that happen," Kennin said.

"So how'd the car handle, anyway?" Angelita asked, changing the subject.

"Really good," Kennin answered. "I mean, I couldn't get a sense for what she'd feel like flat out because the road was wet, but it felt good. I just hope I get to try it on dry road sometime."

"I don't see why you wouldn't," Angelita said.

The rain was coming down even harder now. The 240's wipers swept back and forth across the windshield. The inside of the SX was steamy from their wet hair and clothes. Angelita had to turn on the defroster to clear the fogged glass. Coming toward them in the distance was a set of flashing yellow lights.

"The wrecker for Driftdog," Tito muttered.

The yellow lights grew larger and brighter until the tow truck passed them. They rode most of the rest of the way home in silence, the inside of the car warm and moist. But it was quiet only because the guys couldn't hear the debate raging in Angelita's head as she drove. Ever since she'd seen that look on Mariel's face, she'd been overwhelmed by unexpected feelings of jealousy. She could not let that *puta* have Kennin. She just couldn't.

By the time they reached the city limits, it was pouring. Whoever designed the drainage system for the streets of Las Vegas had not been thinking much about runoff in the desert. The water was nearly six inches deep in some of the intersections they drove through.

They stopped in front of Rivera's Service Center. The lights were off and the place was dark. Streetlights were few and far between in this part of town, and the wet pavement glistened under the 240 SX's headlights. For a moment they sat in the car.

"Interesting evening," Kennin finally said to Angelita. "Thanks for giving me the chance." He started to reach for the door handle.

Suddenly Angelita realized she didn't want him to go. At least, not yet. "Wait. How're you going to get home?"

To Kennin the answer was obvious: the same way he always did. "Take a bus," he said, although he wasn't looking forward to walking through the rain to the bus stop.

"You'll get soaked," Angelita said.

Kennin shrugged. It hardly mattered. He was already soaked.

Angelita turned to her brother. "Tito, could you leave us alone for a moment?"

"Why?" Tito asked from the back.

"I want to talk to Kennin about something," Angelita said. "In private."

"Well, excuuuse me," Tito said in a huff, and clapped

his hand on Kennin's shoulder. "Catch you later, _amigo._"

Kennin leaned forward in the passenger seat. Tito climbed past him and got out. He ran across the sidewalk through the rain and into the garage.

"Why don't you let me give you a ride home?" Angelita asked once her brother was gone.

"It's pretty far out of the way," Kennin said.

"It's fifteen minutes," Angelita said. She waited for his answer. When he said nothing, she added, "I know where you live."

Rain pelted the roof. A car passed and splashed through a puddle. Kennin said nothing. In the silence, Angelita began to feel bad. "It's not like I've been spying on you or anything. But that night you said you had to change buses, I knew there were no other routes out there. You must have been going someplace where you could walk."

Kennin nodded but still said nothing. Angelita was worried he might be angry. "So what do you say?" she asked.

"It's not the way it seems," he said.

"I'm not sure what you mean by that," she said.

"I mean . . ." He paused and sighed. "Look, it doesn't matter. Sure, I'll take a ride home. That's really nice of you."

The rain was still roaring down. Tito was waiting for them just inside the open garage door. Angelita rolled down her window. "Go ahead," she said. "I'm going to drive Kennin home. I'll be back later."

"Can't I—," Tito began to say.

It seemed to Kennin that Tito was going to ask if he could go too. Angelita's face was turned away from Kennin so he couldn't see what happened, only that Tito quickly appeared to change his mind and waved good-bye.

Angelita started to drive. The rain pelted the roof and hood. The windshield wipers slashed back and forth across the glass. The streets of Las Vegas were almost empty, as if the locals couldn't cope with the combined hazards of the dark and the rain.

"Does Tito know?" Kennin asked.

"Where you live?" Angelita said. "No. I won't tell him if you don't want me to."

"Thanks," Kennin said.

They splashed through puddles. It rained so rarely in Las Vegas that each splash caught Angelita by surprise. It reminded her of the tsuiso Kennin had run that night.

"You held back on purpose tonight," she said.

"I did what I needed to do," Kennin answered.

"You knew if you jumped out to a big lead Ian would take too many chances trying to catch up," Angelita said. "And he could have crashed like Driftdog did."

"Was it that obvious?" Kennin asked.

"I don't know about anyone else, but it was to me," she said.

"To Ian, too," said Kennin. "At the finish he was royally pissed off. Said I wasn't even drifting and that our heat shouldn't have counted."

"Meanwhile, you were doing him a big favor," said Angelita. "And him, of all people."

"You mean, because he's a racist?" Kennin said.

"Didn't you think for just one moment that the world might be better off without him?" Angelita asked.

"Not by my hand," Kennin said.

"People crash on wet mountain roads all the time," said Angelita. "Even when they're not drifting."

He turned and stared at her. "You serious? You really think I should have done that?"

"No." She smiled. "Just a fantasy."

He turned away and stared out the rain-streaked side window. "Sometimes it's not a fantasy."

The windshield wipers swished back and forth.

"Anyone you know?" Angelita asked.

The question caught Kennin by surprise. He turned and looked at her again. "What do you mean?"

"Earlier tonight when Tito asked you about drifting in the rain," she said. "There was something about the way you answered. And just now. It's like a weight pulling you down."

Kennin felt his eyebrows rise. He hadn't realized how perceptive she was. "Yeah, maybe something happened."

"A friend?" she asked.

Kennin nodded.

"You know, it's something I've never understood," Angelita said. "The way so many of these guys think they're invincible. I mean, the stories you hear about them drinking and driving, or going out and hitting a hundred and thirty, a hundred and forty in their overpowered crappy cars. . . . And you know there's no possible way they could stop in time if there was something unexpected in the roadway. . . . Or drifting in and out of parked cars in parking lots. It's like they're either in a dream world or they're really crazy."

Kennin nodded. He'd known that dream world well. Only it wasn't a dream when someone you knew died. And not a nightmare either. Because with a nightmare you woke up sooner or later and it was over. Doug was gone, but the memory of him was still there, day after day, reminding Kennin of what his careless mistake had cost.

Raindrops peppered the windshield. Through the blur Kennin made out the twin dead palm trees that marked the entrance to the Sierra Ne-vue.

"It's up ahead on the right," he said.

The words caught Angelita by surprise. They'd gotten there too fast. She hadn't had time to steer the conversation where she'd hoped it would go. Instead she'd gotten sidetracked talking about boys thinking they were invincible. Now she pulled into the trailer park, having gotten nowhere with Kennin. Rainwater dripped from the dead brown fronds of the trees, and the front right tire of the 240 SX unexpectedly dropped as it splashed into a water-filled pothole. Even though she'd always heard this was a bad neighborhood, she was surprised by how run-down it was.

"It's that one." Kennin pointed at his trailer. The windows were dark and Shinchou's yellow Corolla was parked outside. Kennin knew his sister had not yet returned from Los Angeles. Angelita pulled up next to the Corolla.

For a few moments they sat in the car with the engine running, the rain pattering against the roof of the car and the wipers swiping back and forth. In the moist, warm air, Kennin once again became aware of Angelita's perfume.

"Thanks for the ride," he said.

Angelita felt a sensation almost like panic. He would get out of the car now and next week in school there'd be Mariel. *And Mariel always got what she wanted. . . .*

"Wait." Angelita put her hand on his arm. Kennin looked down at it and then at her, curiously.

The words that followed were some of the most difficult Angelita had ever spoken. "Maybe I . . . could come in?"

6

"Whoa! What have we here?"

Kennin was in the bathroom of the trailer the next morning when he heard an obnoxious laugh and the grating sound of Jack the jackass's voice. He pushed open the bathroom door and saw his sister, Shinchou, and Jack standing in the doorway of his sister's bedroom. Jack the jackass was Shinchou's boyfriend, nearly twice her age and a complete jerk. As usual, he was dressed in black, with a black cowboy hat and lots of heavy gold jewelry. Kennin noticed that his sister looked different somehow, but he didn't have time to focus on what about her had changed. He quickly left the bathroom and headed toward Jack.

"Hey, how about some privacy, okay?" Kennin said.

Shinchou and Jack the jackass turned toward him with surprised looks on their faces.

"Just close the door," Kennin said. "I'll explain."

Shinchou closed her bedroom door and Kennin led them into the dining area of the trailer. By now he had figured out what was different about his sister. Her chest was about four times larger than it had been before. He also understood now what Shinchou had been doing in Los Angeles for the past week.

Kennin caught his sister's eye. Shinchou quickly looked away, as if she were unable to meet his gaze.

"She's a friend of mine," Kennin said, referring to Angelita, who'd spent the night in Shinchou's bed. "She gave me a ride home last night because it was raining, and then we talked for a while. It got late, so I told her to stay."

Jack the jackass gave him a leering, dubious look and glanced at the small couch in the dining area of the trailer where Kennin usually slept.

"So how was Los Angeles?" Kennin asked to change the subject.

"Good, good," Jack said, and glanced at Shinchou. "We accomplished a lot, didn't we, sweetheart?"

Shinchou nodded, but hung her head and stared at the floor.

"Well, I guess I better get going. Got a lot to catch up on," Jack said, and turned to Shinchou. "Now, you know what to do. Take it easy for a few days and follow the doctor's orders."

Shinchou didn't react. Jack frowned, then turned to

Kennin. "She'll be okay. She just needs to rest. Once she's feeling better and gets back to work, things are gonna change for you two. And I mean for the better."

The jackass made it sound like he'd done Kennin and his sister a huge favor, but Kennin seriously doubted that. Jack the jackass wasn't the sort of fellow who did anything for anyone unless he stood to benefit the most. Kennin waited for him to leave. A moment later from outside came the sound of Jack's 'vette revving, then the crunch of gravel under tires. Kennin glanced at his sister. She looked tired and uneasy and still wouldn't meet his gaze. A wave of anger rose up inside Kennin. He was angry at Jack for using his sister, and angry at Shinchou for allowing herself to be used. But he forced the anger down. There was no point in it. What was done, was done.

"You okay?" he asked his sister.

She shrugged. A tear rolled down her cheek.

"Anything I can do?" he asked.

She shook her head and looked away as more tears followed. Kennin went to the bedroom door and knocked. "Angelita?"

"I'll be out in a second," she called back.

In awkward silence he waited by the bedroom door, not knowing what to say. Shinchou dabbed the tears off her face and stood up slowly, grimacing. It was obvious that she was in pain. The bedroom door opened and Angelita came out. She stopped when she saw Shinchou.

"Angelita Rivera, this is my sister, Shinchou," Kennin said. "Shinchou, this is my friend Angelita."

"I hope it's okay that I stayed in your room," Angelita said uncomfortably.

"It's fine. I don't mind," Shinchou said. "Nice to meet you." She went past them and into her room, closing the door firmly behind her. Angelita gave Kennin a puzzled look.

"Give me a second, okay?" Kennin said.

"I'll wait outside," Angelita said.

Kennin knocked softly on the bedroom door. He could hear his sister sobbing inside. "Shin?"

His sister didn't answer.

"Listen, I gotta go to work," Kennin said. "Is there anything I can do before I go?"

Still no answer.

"Okay, I'll try to come straight home after work," Kennin said. "You know the number at the Babylon, so if you need anything, just call, okay?"

Silence. Kennin hated to leave her like that, but he knew he had to get to work. "Shin?"

Finally, from inside the room, came her answer, a plain and simple "Thanks."

Kennin left the trailer. After the hard rain the night before, the colors looked brighter, the sky bluer, the weeds greener, the dead palm fronds browner. The air was clear and smelled fresh. Angelita was waiting for him in her car. Kennin got in.

"Is she okay?" Angelita asked.

"I hope," Kennin said, feeling the anger welling up inside again.

"Who was that guy?"

"Jack the jackass. The king of all jerks."

"Her boyfriend?"

"How'd you guess?"

"He looked like bad news."

"Yeah, and it just got worse."

Angelita knew they were simply making conversation to avoid the real conversation. "So where are we going?"

"Can you give me a ride downtown?" Kennin asked.

"Sure."

She drove him downtown. Angelita was dying to talk about the previous night. She wanted to ask him what it meant. She wanted to know what he thought. What he was thinking right now. What he might be thinking about the future. *Their* future. Of course she couldn't ask.

So they rode in silence. After the previous night's rain, the bright clear sunlight seemed to make everything sparkle. On the strip the windows and street signs, even the city buses, seemed cleaner than Kennin remembered.

They pulled up in front of the parking garage at the Babylon Casino. It was still early, and Kennin was glad no one was around. Getting dropped off in the morning by a babe was a certain invitation for some serious razzing by the guys he worked with. Still sitting in the car, he turned to Angelita and said, "Thanks for the ride."

Angelita took a deep breath and mustered her strength. "About last night."

"I really enjoyed spending time with you," Kennin said.

A wave of relief swept through Angelita and she tried not to let her smile appear too broad. "Me too."

"Catch you later, okay?" Kennin said.

"Sure."

Kennin got out of the car. He was just closing the door when Tito came around the corner on his BMX. Angelita's brother froze and his eyes got wide. Kennin watched as Angelita drove off without noticing her brother. Meanwhile, on the sidewalk, Tito got off his bike and shook his head as if coming out of a state of shock. With his face turning red, he stomped toward Kennin, his eyes narrowed and his hands balled into fists. "*Carajo!* That was *mi hermana*!"

Knowing his friend was all bluster, Kennin sighed. "Yeah, Tito, I think I knew that."

"What'd you do?" Tito demanded angrily.

"Calm down," Kennin said.

But Tito wouldn't be mollified. "You spent the night with her?" he yelled, loudly enough for several people on the sidewalk to turn and look at them.

"She spent the night at my place, yes," Kennin said.

"Did anything happen?" Tito demanded.

What did or didn't happen was none of Tito's business, but Kennin knew that telling him would only make things worse. "Come on, Tito, chill. What do you want me to say?"

"I want to know what happened," Tito shouted.

"We talked for a long time," Kennin said.

"Is that *all*?"

Kennin sighed again. More people were staring at them. "Let's go inside, okay?" He started through the entrance to the parking garage. Tito followed, pushing his bike and still talking way too loudly. "*Mi madre* had a world-class fit last night," he said. "I mean, congratulations, dude, that's the first time my sister's ever stayed out all night."

Kennin stopped and turned. "Angelita called her to say where she was. I know she did because I was there."

"So what?" Tito yelled. "What does that matter? She didn't come home, dude. That's the only thing that matters."

"Excuse me, guys." Tony, the head of valet parking, came out of the garage office. He was frowning. "Kennin, there's someone in the office who wants to talk to you."

Kennin looked past Tony and into the office. Detective Neilson of the Las Vegas police was standing by the punch-in clock, studying the time cards. Kennin felt a chill creep down his spine.

Tony dropped his voice. "You in trouble?"

7

Kennin shrugged. "Not sure."

"Better go in and see what he wants," Tony said.

Kennin stepped into the valet parking office. It was still early and the key board had only a few keys on it. Out of habit, he glanced at the bank of black-and-white monitors and saw that only the first two floors of the parking garage were filled. But if this was like any other Sunday, by three that afternoon the garage would be packed.

Detective Neilson was a heavyset man with short blond hair and a trimmed blond mustache. When Kennin entered the office, the detective gestured for him to take a seat. Kennin knew the drill. The cops always wanted you sitting while they stood. It was a power thing, meant to intimidate.

"So what's cookin'?" Neilson asked.

"I figured you'd tell me," Kennin replied. "That's why you're here, isn't it?"

"Funny, I thought you'd know why I was here," said Neilson.

Kennin frowned. He truly had no idea. The last time they'd seen each other it had been to discuss the matter of a stolen car. But that should have been old news by now.

"You know, we still haven't figured out who boosted that GTO," Neilson said.

"Wasn't me," Kennin said.

Neilson nodded in a way that seemed to imply that he wasn't certain he believed that. "Sooner or later we'll find out. You know how it works, don't you, Kennin? One of these days we'll pick up some punk who's looking at time and he'll want to negotiate, you know? They always do. So we'll ask him what he's got, and lo and behold, he'll know something about this GTO that was boosted. At that point, it'll be up to us to decide whether to follow the lead, understand?"

Kennin nodded. "Question. Just out of curiosity, okay? There must be a hundred cars a night stolen in this city. What's the big deal?"

"Turns out that GTO belonged to the mayor's wife," Neilson said. "She got bent out of shape and yelled at the mayor. So he yelled at the chief of police. And from there it went down the ranks to little old me."

"So, basically, someone took the wrong car?" Kennin asked.

"Right," Neilson replied. "And now it's my problem. But like I said, these things have a way of coming full circle.

Sooner or later we'll get the lead we're looking for. And then it'll be up to us to decide whether to follow it. Maybe we will and maybe we won't. Depends on the circumstances."

By now Kennin understood. Neilson was there to make a deal. He wanted something, and if Kennin gave it to him, the matter of the boosted GTO might be forgotten for good.

"I think I see where this is going," Kennin said.

"Word on the street this morning's that there was some racing in the mountains again last night."

"Serious? In the rain?" Kennin pretended to be surprised, but he knew he wasn't fooling the detective.

"Yeah, serious," Neilson said. "Some idiot banged up his car pretty good. It's a miracle that no one was killed. I mean, racing at night in the mountains in the rain? That's a sure recipe for disaster. You gotta have the brains of a frickin' tree stump to try that crap."

Knowing the detective was trying to get a rise out of him, Kennin merely nodded. "I couldn't agree more, sir."

Neilson set his jaw and leaned toward him. It was time to get down to business. "Look, Kennin, just between you and me, if people want to go out and risk their necks doing stupid things, there's not a lot the Las Vegas PD can do about it. We got all kinds of crazies around here. Skydivers, animal trainers, poisonous snake collectors, you name it. The thing is, those people aren't putting anyone else's life in danger, understand? But when guys are racing on mountain roads, they're not just risking their own lives; they're risking the lives of the innocent people who drive on those roads as well. And that is something the Las Vegas PD can do something about. In fact, it's something we *have* to do something about."

From outside came a faint, smooth, high-pitched whine. Kennin recognized it immediately. It was the Ferrari Scaglietti of Mike Mercado, the owner of the Babylon Casino. From the sound, Kennin figured the car was still half a block away. The last thing Kennin needed was for Mercado to see him in the garage office with this detective.

"And your point is?" Kennin said to Neilson, hoping to hurry him along.

Neilson slid his hands into his pockets. "Look, this kind of racing they do. It's called drifting, right?"

"If you say so," Kennin replied, knowing better than to act like he knew anything about it.

"From what I've read, it started over in Japan or some-place," said Neilson.

"Oh yeah?" Kennin didn't quite see what that had to do with anything.

Neilson said nothing. He just gazed steadily at him. Kennin blinked as the implication sank in. "Wait a minute. Are you saying that because I'm half Japanese that I'm somehow responsible for it?"

Neilson bristled, narrowing his eyes. "I don't know. But I've spent my career working with young guys like you, okay? After a while you learn to spot types. This may surprise you,

Kennin, but it's pretty much the same story over and over. There are a couple of leaders and the rest are followers. It took me about a minute to make you for one of the leaders. Now I got a real simple job, my friend. My boss tells me what to do and I do it. And right now my boss is telling me to get the road racers off the roads. Got it?"

Kennin nodded, even though he was only listening with one ear. The other ear was monitoring the approach of the Ferrari.

"Now, you want it simple?" Neilson went on. "One of these days I'm gonna get some information that'll connect you to that boosted GTO. And when that day comes, I'll be looking back to see how cooperative you were on this drifting thing. If we still got a problem with kids racing in the mountains at night, I can pretty much promise that you'll be spending a lot more time around prison than those weekly visits you pay your old man over at Nellis."

Kennin nodded, but the words didn't really sink in. Outside, the metallic blue Ferrari Scaglietti pulled into the garage. Mike Mercado got out and stared into the valet parking office at Kennin.

"I'm serious, Kennin," Neilson said, as if he sensed he didn't have Kennin's full attention. "From now on I'm gonna be on your ass like a fly on manure. And I'm gonna stay there until this thing's over, one way or another. So do yourself a favor. Set an example for the rest of the guys. You get them off the streets, you might just get me off your back."

Kennin didn't mean to be disrespectful, especially to anyone packing a detective's badge. But it was hard to stay focused when Neilson was issuing empty threats and Mike Mercado was staring into the office, no doubt wondering what Kennin had done to bring the cops sniffing around.

"You hear me, Kennin?" Neilson finally asked.

"Loud and clear, sir."

Neilson left the office. Kennin remained inside. Outside, Mike Mercado stopped the detective. Kennin couldn't hear what the casino owner said, but he saw Mercado's lips move. It was pretty easy to figure out that Mercado was asking what was going on. They finished speaking, and Neilson got into his car and left.

Now Kennin got up. Out in the parking garage, Mercado and Tony were waiting for him. Tito was standing off to the side with a big frown, still pissed about Angelita spending the night with his friend. Kennin expected to get grilled by the casino boss, so he was caught off guard when Mercado said to Tony, "Think I can borrow these two kids for a little while?"

Tony looked as surprised as any of them. "Sure, Mr. Mercado, whatever you like."

Mike Mercado turned to Tito and Kennin. "You two, come with me."

8

Tito and Kennin followed Mercado into the casino. Tito gave Kennin an icy but quizzical look, asking if he had any idea what was going on. Kennin shrugged his shoulders and tipped his head as if to say, *Just do what the boss says.* Normally they would have walked together, but this time Tito made sure to distance himself from Kennin, letting him know he was still supremely pissed about his sister.

While it wasn't particularly hot outside, the atmosphere inside the casino was air-conditioned to cool, dry perfection. The walls were lined with mirrors and gilt-framed paintings of seminude women. They walked past the banks of elevators where gamblers and guests waited to go to other floors. To their left was the vast, glittering, noisy casino with its endless rows of slot machines and gambling tables covered by green felt. People around the elevator recognized

Mercado. Some waved. Some nodded. A few called out, "Hey, Mr. Mercado."

Mike Mercado responded to each of them with a terse nod and led Kennin and Tito to a small elevator that required a key to open. Unlike the public elevators, this one had no light-up numbers over the doors to indicate which floors it went to. The gold doors opened, and Mercado gestured for Tito and Kennin to enter. Inside, Mercado again used the key, this time to turn a lock beside the letters PH.

The elevator began to rise. Tito stood behind Mercado. Still keeping his distance, he gave Kennin a frown and gestured at the PH. Kennin silently mouthed the word "penthouse." Tito's eyes widened.

The elevator stopped and the doors opened into a dark, wood-paneled office. An attractive blond woman wearing glasses sat at a desk, typing on a silver laptop computer.

"Hello, Laney," Mercado said to the blonde.

"Hello, Mr. Mercado," the secretary answered in a British accent.

"Anything important?" the casino owner asked.

Laney handed him a dark red folder. "Last night's take. Security report. Dinner invitations. Charity solicitations. An invitation from the Automobile Club De l'Ouest."

Mercado stopped. "Le Mans?"

"I believe so, sir."

"Great." Mercado smiled broadly, slid the folder under his arm, and headed toward two large dark wooden doors that opened into an enormous office lined with dark red curtains. Tito and Kennin hesitated by the doors, not knowing whether Mercado wanted them to follow. The casino owner turned and waved. "Come on."

The boys followed him. On one side of the office was a bar, a black leather couch and chairs, and an entertainment center with a huge flat-screen TV. On the other side of the room was a Ping-Pong table, and against the wall, an enormous fish tank was filled with colorful tropical fish. Near the far wall was a huge shiny black desk with two computers, phones, and models of sleek sports and racing cars.

And dead center in the middle of the office, standing like a shrine to the god of speed, was the sleekest red, white, and chrome motorcycle either Tito or Kennin had ever seen. If Tito's eyes had grown any bigger they would have popped right out of his head.

Mercado sat down at the desk. "Have a look around while I take care of a few things," he said.

While the casino owner went through the red folder and made some phone calls, Tito and Kennin went their separate ways. Kennin's first stop was the motorcycle. It was gorgeous, sleek and streamlined, polished until it practically glowed.

At his desk Mercado put his hand over the phone. "It's a Ducati Desmosedici."

Kennin had never heard of it, but somehow, he wasn't surprised. Like the Scaglietti, this motorcycle came from a world of ultragorgeous design and engineering that regular mortals rarely got to see. After the motorcycle, Kennin checked out the entertainment center and the fish tank. But wherever he went, he could feel Mercado's eyes on him. When he stopped near the dark red curtains, curious to see what was on the other side, Mercado pushed a button on his desk. With a faint electric hum, the curtains began to open and bright sunlight spread into the room. The next thing Kennin knew, he was squinting out at Las Vegas, the Great Basin, and the mountains that surrounded it.

"Nice view, huh?" Mercado asked from his desk.

Tito had been looking at the Ducati when Mercado opened the shades. "Why don't you keep the windows open all the time?" he asked.

"I'd never get any work done," the casino owner replied.

"You mean," Tito stammered, looking around the vast room. "This is . . . your office?"

"What did you think it was?" Mercado asked.

"I don't know," Tito said. "I guess I thought maybe you lived here or something."

Mercado chuckled. "Come on, boys." He stood up and waved at them to join him at the couch and chairs in front of the entertainment center.

"Have a seat," the casino owner said. "Thirsty?"

"Uh, yeah," said Tito.

Kennin sat on the black couch. It was leather, but not like any leather he'd ever felt before. This was soft and smooth, almost buttery to the touch. Meanwhile, Tito chose to sit farther from Kennin than he normally would have.

Mercado pressed a button on a small intercom on the coffee table. "Laney?"

"Yes, Mr. Mercado?"

"Could you come in here, please?"

The door opened and the beautiful blond secretary came in.

"What would you like, boys?" Mercado asked.

"Uh, a Coke for me," Tito said.

"Me too," said Kennin.

"Make that three Cokes," said Mercado.

Laney went to the bar to pour the drinks. Mercado sat down on the couch and crossed one leg over the other. His black shoes shone. "Now, just to get something out of the way, the reason the Ducati is up here is because I had to find a place to keep it where I wouldn't be tempted to ride it."

"Why not?" asked Tito.

"Because it's the world's fastest motorcycle," the casino owner explained. "Some people will argue that the Suzuki Hayabusa is faster, but as you boys may have noticed, I have a special place in my heart for Italian engineering."

"So why's it up here?" Kennin asked.

"Everyone's got a weakness, and mine is speed,"

Mercado explained. "I figure as long as I'm in a car, I have half a chance of surviving." He pointed at the Ducati. "Put me on that thing on an open road, and I'm in trouble."

Kennin glanced down at the coffee table. On display were small models of racing cars as well as a photo of Mercado in a racing suit, his forehead glistening with sweat, an open bottle of champagne in one hand and a winner's trophy in the other. Mercado saw him looking.

"It was just a small GT event over at Spring Lake," the casino owner said.

"You get to race much?" Kennin asked.

"Not enough to be good at it," Mercado replied. "The guys at the top run every week." He paused and smiled as if he'd just thought of something. "Wouldn't you agree?"

Kennin rarely if ever felt his face grow hot, but now he felt a blush spread across his cheeks. Laney served the soda in heavy glass tumblers filled with ice, each glass set on a silver coaster on the table. Tito and Kennin thanked her.

Mercado took a sip. "The word on the street is you're pretty good at this drifting business."

"Don't believe everything you hear," Kennin said.

Mercado turned his gaze to Tito.

"He's okay," Tito said with a begrudging shrug.

Mercado nodded in a way that seemed to indicate that he suspected there was a little too much modesty in the room. "I know this drifting stuff originated on winding mountain roads, but suppose someone wanted to make it legitimate? How would you go about doing that? Like at a track where people would pay to see it?"

"Piece of cake!" Tito answered so quickly and eagerly that it caught Kennin by surprise. "You don't even need a track. You could do it in a parking lot. You just set out the course with cones, or if you really want to get fancy, line it with hay bales. People could sit up in bleachers and have a view of the whole course. I mean, you wouldn't believe how easy it would be."

"I guess you've given this some thought," Mercado said.

"Damn straight!" Tito blurted, then colored. "Er, I mean, yes, Mr. Mercado, I have given it some thought."

Mike Mercado smiled. "Good. I like enthusiasm." He turned to Kennin. "What do you think?"

Kennin knew he had to keep his opinions to himself, especially when it came to organized car racing. He was a street racer, plain and simple. He didn't like ovals or tracks. He didn't like crowds. He despised "officials" telling him what to do. He raced for himself, not for an audience that was mostly interested in crashes and near misses.

Instead, he said, "I guess it would work. The problem with a lot of road racing is that no matter where you are, you can't see the whole course. You have to stand in one place and only get to watch the cars when they go by."

"Or you're in an oval track, NASCAR-type situation,"

Tito added. "Just watching the cars go around and around. Which can get kind of boring."

"Or drag racing," said Mercado.

"Right," said Tito. "I mean, I like all those forms of racing. But the thing about drifting is it's run in two-car heats, so you can hold the event in a tight space on an overlapping track without having to worry about the cars getting spaced out and T-boning each other."

The intercom on the coffee table buzzed.

"Yes, Laney?" Mercado said.

"Mr. Jamison is here."

"Tell him to come in."

The dark wooden doors opened and Derek Jamison hustled in. He was Mercado's sidekick, but unlike the casino owner, who dressed in neatly pressed, stylish suits, Derek appeared to wear the same wrinkled gray suit and black shirt day after day. "Sorry I'm late. I had to bust a few legs and bury a body out in the desert." He winked at Kennin and Tito. "Just kidding, boys." He strode over to the bar and pulled a bottle of beer out of the fridge, then came over to the coffee table and sat down. "So what'd I miss?"

"The boys were just telling me that they think drifting could be an event with a paid gate," Mercado said.

"What'd I tell you?" said Derek. "Here's the headline: 'Drifting Comes to the Babylon! Catch the action and excitement, the thrills and chills of motorsport's newest competitive event!'"

Mercado gave a nod of approval.

"Excuse me, sir," Kennin said. "There's one thing I don't quite get. This is a casino, not a racetrack. What's the point?"

"Marketing," Mercado answered. "It's like this, Kennin: When it comes right down to it, there's no difference between one casino and the next. On a very basic level, we all offer the same thing—an opportunity to gamble money in order to make more of it."

"Ahem." Derek cleared his throat and winked.

Mercado nodded back. "Of course, everyone knows that the only way casinos stay in business is by taking in more money than they pay out, but that's beside the point. The point is, if we're all offering the public the same thing, why should they gamble here at the Babylon and not at the Bellagio or New York, New York?"

"I don't know, sir," Kennin said. "I guess I just assumed the Babylon was a better casino."

"Good answer, kid," Derek chuckled. "But unfortunately, it ain't the right answer."

"The right answer," said Mercado, "is that in order to stay successful, every casino has to create an illusion, an atmosphere that makes people want to gamble there. So this one offers sexy showgirls, and that one offers world-famous lion tamers. Another casino has a big free buffet dinner, and yet another one offers lots of entertainment for kids and becomes the place for families."

"You want to be the casino for drifters?" Tito asked.

"Not quite," Mercado said with a smile. "We're thinking about becoming the casino for gearheads of all types. We'd feature automotive themes, from car racing to hot rods, motorcycles, monster trucks . . . just about anything that's motorized and on wheels. We'll have all kinds of events, rides, you name it."

"But we like drifting because it's new and different," Derek said. "It's not just another drag race or stock car event. It's the kind of thing that people will be curious about. It could pull a lot of people into the casino."

A phone rang and the intercom on the coffee table blinked. "Mr. Mercado?"

"Yes, Laney?" Mercado answered.

"Mr. Wynn is on line three."

"Tell him I'll call him back in five." Mercado stood, draining his glass of soda. "Kennin, I want to talk to you for a second. In private."

Tito frowned. Kennin followed Mercado across the office. The room was so big that you could walk across it and speak in a low voice and not worry about being heard. They stood beside the windows. In the distance, beyond Glitter Gulch, was Nellis Air Force Base, which also housed the prison camp where Kennin's father was doing time. Beyond that was Sperling Mountain, where the drifters had run in the rain the night before.

Mercado faced the window and spoke in a low voice.

Kennin realized he didn't want Derek or Tito to see his lips. "So what's the story with that police detective?"

Kennin told him the truth: that he and Tito had found themselves in a stolen GTO being driven by Tito's dim-witted cousin Raoul, and when Raoul got too drunk to drive, Kennin had "disposed" of the vehicle.

Mercado pressed his fingers into a tent and looked thoughtful. "One thing about the casino business, Kennin. People are always looking for a connection between us and the bad guys. Granted, they have good reason. Up till recently the business was strictly mob run. But that's changed. The gaming commission smells any connection to the mob now and you can lose your casino license. That's serious stuff, understand?"

Kennin nodded slowly.

"Normally, I'd hear a story like that, and given what happened with you and my car the other day, that would be the end of you," Mercado said.

Kennin winced at the memory of being caught by Mercado late one night taking the Scaglietti for a joy ride through the Babylon parking garage. It was the sort of thing that could result in a nasty beating by casino security, but Mercado had let him off with a stern warning because Kennin had been honest.

"But I also hear you're the most talented drifter around," Mercado went on. "If this drifting thing is gonna work, I'm gonna need you. But you gotta stay out of trouble, understand? 'Cause next time there ain't gonna be a next time."

"I understand," Kennin said.

Mercado put his hand on Kennin's shoulder and steered him back toward Derek and Tito. "So here's the story, boys. I'm putting Derek in charge. He'll be in touch with you."

Mercado walked Tito and Kennin to the office doors. "Think you guys can find your way back without me?" the casino owner asked.

"I'll make sure Tito doesn't wind up in the cocktail lounge," Kennin joked.

Mercado grinned, but Tito frowned as if trying to remind Kennin that he was still angry about Angelita. Mercado opened the door for them. "Okay, boys, Derek will let you know what we decide to do."

Tito and Kennin went out. The private elevator was waiting with the door open. Laney rose from her desk with a key and motioned the boys into the elevator. She keyed the lock and the doors closed.

The elevator started to descend. Tito stared at the door and didn't say a word. When they got to the ground floor, he stepped out and went ahead, leaving Kennin behind.

By now Kennin had had enough. "Hey, Tito, wait up."

Tito stopped and crossed his arms.

"How long you gonna keep this up?" Kennin asked.

"I don't want you messing with my sister," Tito answered.

"She's a year older than you," Kennin said. "I think she knows what she's doing, okay?"

"Wrong," Tito said. "Maybe my sister knows what she's doing in school. Maybe she knows cars, so she fixes them up and sells them so she'll have money for college next year. When she goes, she'll be the first person in our family ever to get beyond a high school diploma. But that can't happen if she doesn't go, okay? And that's the problem. She knows a lot about some things, but she's kind of in the dark about others."

"And?" Kennin couldn't figure out where Tito was going with this. Meanwhile, he could tell from Tito's expression that his friend thought it was obvious.

"So, don't take this the wrong way, okay?" Tito said. "You're my friend and a real stand-up guy."

"But . . . ," Kennin prompted him.

"But . . . well . . . no offense or anything, but you hardly make it to school most days," Tito said. "And let's not forget that you're a year younger than her, okay? So you won't be graduating for a least another year. And that's if you graduate at all."

When Kennin realized what Tito was trying to say, it came as a shock. "I'm not good enough for your sister?"

Tito stared down at the floor and then back up at Kennin. "Look, in a lot of ways you're a great guy. Better than most of the jerks around here who are gonna go to college someday. It's not that you're not good enough, okay? It's just that maybe you're not the right guy, okay? There's a difference between being a great guy and being the right guy, understand?"

"I do now," Kennin said.

9

When Kennin got home that night, Shinchou was lying on the couch watching TV. She was wearing a bulky, loose-fitting white terry-cloth robe. On the table beside the couch were bottles of pills, an ashtray with a few butts in it, a small bottle of Mountain Dew, a paper cup with a straw, and packages of gauze pads and bandages.

"How are you feeling?" Kennin asked.

"Sore," his sister answered, then slowly and carefully reached for the paper cup with the straw. Kennin saw her wince.

"I'll get it," he said and held the cup so that his sister could sip through the straw. He'd been surprised when he saw the small bottle of Mountain Dew. Usually they bought soda in the two-liter size to save money. But now he understood that the large size would be too heavy for his sister to handle in her current state.

"Thanks," Shinchou said when she'd finished the drink.

Kennin put the glass down. "Anything else I can do?"

"Could you change the channel? If I have to watch another minute of *Oprah* I think I'll puke."

Kennin flipped through the channels and settled on an old *Fresh Prince of Bel-Air*. "How's that?"

"Fine, thanks." Shinchou settled a little more comfortably into the couch.

"Hungry?" Kennin asked.

Shinchou smiled faintly as if she appreciated his effort to help. "No, thanks. The painkillers do a really good job of killing my appetite."

Kennin sat down on a chair. On the TV, Jazz was trying to explain that even though the label on the shrunken shirt had said "Hand wash," he had put it in the drier because he'd washed his hands.

Kennin and his sister laughed, then Shinchou grimaced in pain. "It hurts to laugh. You gotta change the channel again, Kennin."

Kennin got up and switched the channel to *CSI: Miami*. "Better?"

"Yeah, thanks."

Kennin settled back into the chair. "So how long are you supposed to rest?"

"Another week," she said.

Based on how little she could move, Kennin wondered

if she might need a longer recovery time before she started to "dance" again. "You sure that's enough?"

Shinchou made a face. "It's all I can afford to take."

Kennin gave her a puzzled look. "I don't follow."

"I have to go back to work," his sister said.

"What if you're not ready?" he asked.

Shinchou slowly shook her head. "It doesn't work that way. It's already been a week and by then it'll be two. We need to pay the rent and the TV bill and buy food. And Jack wants his money back."

This was the first time Shinchou had said anything about owing Jack money, but it made sense. How else could she have afforded the trip to LA and the "procedure" she'd had done?

"How much?" Kennin asked.

Shinchou winced as if she didn't want to say. "A lot."

"Come on."

She let out a sigh. "Five grand."

Kennin caught his breath. Five thousand dollars was a huge amount of money. He couldn't imagine how his sister was supposed to come up with it. "Does he want interest on top of it?"

Shinchou stared at the TV and didn't answer, but the muscles in her face had grown tight. Kennin felt a pang. He knew what that expression meant. Jack the jackass had a tight grip on his sister now. With Shinchou owing interest on top of the five grand, it would take forever for her to pay him back. He could keep her working at the "gentlemen's club" for as long as he wanted.

"I know what you're thinking," his sister said without looking away from the TV. "You think Jack had it planned from the start. But it's not true. I don't have to work at Rustler's if I don't want to. I can work at any club I want."

"As long as you pay him back with interest," Kennin said.

"Of course," Shinchou said. "Don't forget, Jack's a businessman. And this is his business."

"I thought you were his girlfriend," Kennin said. "Not his business."

Shinchou stared at the TV and didn't answer.

10

Maybe Kennin was imagining it, but it seemed like the atmosphere in school was tense the next morning. It was the way people he barely knew stared at him for an extra moment in the hall, or grew quiet when he passed.

He was on his way to lunch when someone behind him called, "Hey, wait up."

Kennin turned. Megs, the tall, thin blond kid who helped run the tsuisos, hurried toward him. As usual, he was wearing his red and black racing jacket.

"'Sup, Kennin?" They slapped hands.

"Not much," Kennin said.

"Really sucked the other night, huh?" said Megs.

"You mean, the rain?"

"Yeah," Megs said. "Frickin' Driftdog, you know?"

"It's bad news," said Kennin. "But it seems like he always bounces back."

"Yeah, well, you know how it is," Megs said. "When you live to drift and drift to live, you do whatever you have to do to be ready for the next battle. That guy would probably drift in his mother's minivan if he had to."

Kennin grinned. The image of Driftdog Dave in a minivan screaming sideways around a corner was pretty amusing. He and Megs continued toward the cafeteria, but Kennin could tell there was something on Megs's mind.

"So listen," Megs finally said. "You heard what's going on with Ian?"

"No."

"He wants a do-over on Saturday night's tsuiso," Megs said. "He says it wasn't fair because the road was too wet and you didn't drift."

"Crossing the finish line first doesn't count?" Kennin asked.

"It does to me," Megs said. "But I'm not the one who makes the decision. I just want you to know that as far as I'm concerned, you're right. What counts is who wins. Otherwise you'll have guys wanting do-overs because a bug went splat on their windshield."

They turned the corner into the hall that led to the cafeteria. Ahead of them a group of guys was standing just outside the cafeteria doors. Kennin quickly recognized Chris and Ian among them. On the edge of the crowd stood Tito and Mutt, also wearing his red and black racing jacket. The group quieted when Kennin and Megs got near.

"We've been talking about the other night," Chris said. "Some of us think those heats shouldn't count."

Having just heard this news from Megs, Kennin merely nodded.

"Guys think it wasn't a fair heat because of the conditions," Chris went on.

"And because a certain dillweed didn't even bother to drift," added Ian.

Kennin was getting seriously tired of Ian's stupid mouth. "Why bother drifting if there's no need to?" he shot back.

The dis was on the mark and the guys around Ian started to grin. Ian turned red and balled his hands into fists. But rather than strike back at Kennin, he turned to Tito. "Hey, punk, I hear your sister's gonna have a baby with slanty eyes."

The smiles disappeared and the atmosphere in the hall grew tense. The looks came back in Kennin's direction, curious to see what he'd do or say next.

"What is your problem?" Kennin asked.

"My problem's with losers like you who should go back to where they belong," Ian said.

The tension in the air grew thicker. A few guys actually stepped back, as if making room for a fight. But this time Kennin wasn't interested in using his fists.

"And where do we belong?" he asked.

"How would I know?" Ian replied. "Wherever the boat that brought you here left from."

"Seriously, Ian, let me ask you a question," Kennin said. "How long has *your* family been in this country?"

"I don't know," Ian said. "No, wait. My great-grandparents came over. Why? What's that got to do with anything?"

"Where'd they come from?"

"Europe," Ian said.

"And how'd they get here?"

It took a moment, but the other guys in the crowd slowly began to grin. The answer was obvious. People from Ian's great-grandparents' generation came to this country the same way Kennin's grandparents had come—by boat.

Ian glanced around, his face turning red when he saw the grins. He glared at Kennin. "There's one big difference," he sneered. "No one wants your kind around here, gook-a-luke."

Kennin clenched his teeth. The guy had to know there were limits. Lines that shouldn't be crossed. Ian had just crossed a major one. Kennin felt his good intentions drain away. It looked like fists were the only way to deal with this idiot. He stepped toward the red-haired kid.

With unexpected agility for a big guy, Chris slid in front of Kennin and blocked his path. Kennin tried to duck under his arms, but Chris caught him in a bear hug.

Behind Chris, Ian bounced around on his toes like a

boxer with his fists up. "Let him go. Come on, Chris, lemme have a piece of him."

By now, three other guys had gotten between Kennin and Ian, creating a human wall.

"Come on, guys," Ian practically begged. "Watch me whip Japboy's butt."

Kennin struggled against Chris's grip. Meanwhile, Chris said to his pals, "Get him out of here."

Chris's friends seemed to understand that he was talking about Ian, not Kennin. They dragged Ian away into the cafeteria, leaving Chris, Kennin, and a few others out in the hall.

Chris let go of Kennin. "Listen, I got to talk to you in private."

That caught Kennin by surprise. Chris headed for the door next to the cafeteria that led into a courtyard. Kennin followed. The sun was bright and the sky a slightly lighter blue than the day before. It felt warmer, too.

Chris waited until the door had closed behind them. Kennin expected that he wanted to talk about Mariel, so he was surprised when Chris crossed his arms in a serious gesture and said, "Some detective paid me a visit yesterday. He said he talked to you, too."

Kennin nodded.

"You tell him about me?" Chris asked.

Kennin shook his head.

"Then how'd he know?"

"Don't know," Kennin said.

Chris shook his head in disgust. "One thing I hate about this town. Everyone knows everyone's business."

Kennin waited. Chris leveled his gaze at him.

"You don't say much, do you?" Chris said.

"I do when I think it's worth saying," said Kennin.

"We're gonna have to cool this drift thing," Chris said. "I can't have the cops sniffing around. I mean, not with the football team and everything."

Kennin was still wondering what the point of all this was.

"So look," Chris said. "Suppose you and I agree that we don't run for a while, okay? There's some money involved here, and no one wants to get snaked. If both of us agree not to do it, they can't have much of a tsuiso."

Kennin nodded. He wondered if Chris would go so far as to offer his hand for a shake, but that didn't happen. This truce was temporary, and they both knew it.

Without another word, Chris turned and headed back inside. Kennin took his time following. Inside the doors, Tito was waiting for him.

"So?" Tito said.

"So . . . what?" Kennin asked.

"What was that about?" Tito demanded, clearly making no attempt to hide the anger he was still feeling over Angelita.

"It was private, Tito," Kennin said.

"What does that mean?" Tito asked.

"It means I can't talk about it," Kennin said.

"Oh, great, that's just great!" Tito grumbled. "I've got all the jack I own riding on you. First I find out the tsuiso the other night don't count. So we gotta start all over again, and there's that many more chances you'll get beat and I'll lose everything. And now I find out you guys are keeping secrets. Nobody gives a crap about the guy who's got his life savings tied up in this."

Tito was capable of getting pretty dramatic. He probably had a future in the movies. Kennin knew there was no point in trying to remind him that it was his idea to lay those bets down in the first place.

"I didn't say I don't care," Kennin said.

Tito glared at him. "You think I don't see what's going on? First you get my sister. Then you get my money. Man, am I a frickin' idiot, or what? I thought you were my friend."

He turned and stormed down the hall.

11

Nothing could have prepared Angelita for the week that lay ahead. It started on Sunday morning when she got home from Kennin's and her mom went completely ballistic on her for being out all night. Angelita tried to remind her dear *madre* that she was eighteen, and next year she planned to be away at college and living on her own. Would her mother still be checking up on her then? It wasn't the same, her mother screamed. Once Angelita was on her own it would be different, but as long as she lived in the family house, she had to live by the family rules. And rule number one was: Young Women Come Home Every Night!

And if that wasn't enough, there was her brother Tito, glaring at her all through Sunday dinner like she was *una prostituta*. Angelita held her tongue until the two of them were alone in the kitchen cleaning up. Tito was rinsing the dishes and putting them in the dishwasher while she wrapped up the leftovers. He kept glaring at her as if she was lower than a cockroach.

"What?" she finally shouted.

"Nothing," Tito muttered.

"Right. That's why you keep staring at me like I'm dirt," Angelita said.

"Maybe you deserve it," he said.

"Deserve what? What did I do?" Angelita asked.

"You know."

"No, I don't," she said. "Why don't you tell me."

"With my best friend," Tito muttered.

"*What* with your best friend?" Angelita demanded.

Her idiot brother just shook his head and remained tight-lipped.

And still, what happened at home was nothing compared to what she faced at school Monday morning, where every girl she knew—and several she didn't know—either sniggered or snarled or winked at her knowingly.

She was in the girls' room fixing her makeup when her girlfriend Marta came in. Marta was short with long, frizzy, reddish brown hair, pouty lips, and a spunky attitude. She opened her purse and took out a lipstick. The two girls looked at each other in the mirror.

"Making yourself look nice for someone?" Marta asked in a teasing voice.

Angelita rolled her eyes. "Save it, okay? I've been getting it for two days straight and I'm sick of it."

"You serious?" Marta said. "You're the envy of half the girls in school."

"What about the other half?" Angelita asked.

"No problem." Marta winked. "They just hate you."

"It's nobody's business," Angelita said.

"Excuse me?" Marta said. "Hello? We're talking about Dorado High. Everything is everyone's business."

The bathroom door swung open and Mariel Lewis came in with her entourage of wannabes. The bathroom went quiet. Angelita braced herself. It was amazing how the underclass girls immediately backed away from the mirror to give the queen her space. Mariel stepped up to the mirror and began to primp. Her eyes met Angelita's for a split second, and then she went back to applying eyeliner.

Just when Angelita began to let her guard down, Mariel said, "So there's a rumor that you got lucky."

"Don't believe everything you hear," Angelita said.

"Doesn't matter," Mariel said. "It doesn't mean anything anyway."

Angelita caught Marta's eye. She could tell Marta wanted her to come back with some snappy cutdown, but Angelita could see no purpose in doing that. There was nothing to be gained. Girls like Mariel could cut your heart out with their razor tongues. At the same time they seemed to have invisible armor that protected them from even the nastiest comments.

It wasn't easy, but Angelita knew she could deal with

her mother, Tito, and Mariel. It was what happened with Kennin that threw her completely. He seemed to have disappeared from school. Day after day she looked for him in the hall or the library and didn't see him. The one place she didn't want to go was the cafeteria. Because that was where all the gossips were, and she didn't want them to get any more ideas than they already had.

After several days of not seeing him, she finally decided to wait after school. It was a day when she knew he didn't have work at the Babylon, so he would most likely go to the bus stop a few blocks away and take the bus home. She stood behind a tree because she was worried that if he saw her from far away he might change direction. She waited until he was close and then stepped out.

"Hi," she said.

"Oh, hi." Caught by surprise, he forced a smile onto his face.

"How are you?" she asked.

"Okay."

She sensed that something was wrong. It was the way his eyes darted right and left, as if looking for an escape route. He was keeping his distance. Not just physically, but emotionally as well. Could he just be feeling shy? Or was it more than that?

"So . . . haven't seen you around much," she said, hoping that with some encouragement from her he'd warm up.

He averted his eyes. "There's been . . . stuff to do."

Stuff? she thought. So was he saying that as far as he was concerned, "stuff" came before she did?

"I thought I'd . . . I mean, we'd at least talk," she said, hating herself for the feeling of desperation that crept up inside. She began to feel a simmering resentment toward him for forcing her into this position.

He nodded but said nothing, as if he was waiting for her to fill the vacuum. Angelita felt her heart start to sink. As desperately as she wanted to do something to keep it afloat, she stopped herself. She knew from experience that this was no good. There was no point in begging. Kennin had to know what she was looking for, and if he didn't want to give it to her, then she was a fool to keep asking. The last thing she was going to give up was her pride. If she'd made a mistake with him, so be it. She would go away and lick her wounds and to hell with Kennin Burnett.

12

A week passed and Shinchou still wasn't ready to go back to work. She could hardly move around the trailer without wincing in pain. One afternoon Kennin came home from school and found the yellow Corvette parked outside the trailer. Jack the jackass was there.

Kennin let himself into the trailer. Inside, Shinchou was sitting on the couch in her bathrobe. It was still difficult and painful for her to dress. Simply trying to lift her arm higher than her shoulder made her grimace. Her eyes were red, and she was clutching a ball of tissues. Jack was sitting across from her at the small breakfast table. He was wearing sunglasses and a shiny dark suit. His black cowboy hat lay on the table and a cigarette smoldered between his yellowed, nicotine-stained fingers. Unlike almost every other time Kennin had seen him, there was no big turd-eating grin on

Jack's face today. Instead, he looked grim, his lips pressed into a hard, flat line and his eyes hidden behind the dark lenses.

"What's going on?" Kennin asked.

"It's time for sister to get back to work," Jack growled. "Only it seems like she don't want to."

"I can't," Shinchou said with a sniff. "It hurts too much. It hurts to move. It hurts to dance. It hurts to dress. And it's definitely going to hurt to undress."

"Sorry, sister, but I've had plenty of girls back on that stage by now," Jack said. "If they could do it, so can you."

"Not everyone heals at the same pace," Kennin said.

"Yeah, well, that may be true," allowed Jack, "but it's the pace of business I'm thinkin' about. Your sister's forgetting that I got five big ones invested in her, and the vig is getting bigger every day. Now it's real simple. She owes me money and she gotta get to work to pay it back."

"I can't," Shinchou moaned.

"What's vig mean?" Kennin asked.

"It's the interest," Jack said and poked his own chest with his thumb. "This ain't no charity organization, understand? You take a loan from the bank, it's the same thing. They charge interest and so do I."

"You told me I'd have time," Shinchou whimpered.

"You *had* time, but your time's plum run out, sister," Jack snarled. He pointed to the bedroom. "Now go in there and get dressed up really pretty. Then you and I'll go downtown to the Rustler and you can start working off your debt."

Shinchou gave her brother a pleading look. Kennin got the message.

"Not today," Kennin said.

Jack turned his head sharply. "What?"

"I think it's time you left," Kennin said.

Jack looked up at Kennin with a cruel smile on his lips. "Sorry? I don't think I heard you right."

"I think you did," Kennin said.

Jack looked at Shinchou. "Listen up, sister. Your little brother's on the young side. I don't think he knows who he's dealing with. You might want to warn him not to stick his nose where it don't belong."

"Maybe you're the one who doesn't know who you're dealing with," Shinchou replied.

Jack the jackass straightened up. There was no doubt in Kennin's mind that Shinchou's answer was the last thing he'd expected to hear.

"I am disappointed in you, sister," he growled. "I thought you were smarter than this."

"I am not going to ask you again to leave," Kennin said ominously.

"Whoa, and *you* are definitely dumber than I thought, boy," Jack muttered. But at the same time he picked up his black cowboy hat and stood.

Kennin went to the door and held it open for him.

"You kids are new around here," Jack the jackass said, straightening his jacket and taking his time as if to let Kennin know he wasn't intimidated. "It's pretty obvious that you don't have a clue how this town works. So I'll tell you what I'm gonna do, sister. I'm gonna give you a few more days. But then I better see you over at the club. Elsewise you two are gonna be in for a turdstorm the likes of which you ain't never seen."

Kennin was still holding the door open. Jack started through it, then stopped in the doorway. "There's a rumor goin' around that you're some kind of hotshot road-racing driver. Street racing for money. If I were you, I'd be thinkin' about coming up with some of the scratch your sister needs to repay her debts."

Kennin didn't answer. Jack the jackass went out and Kennin let the door close behind him. He and Shinchou listened as the Corvette roared to life and screeched out of the trailer park.

"Thank you." Shinchou dabbed the tears out of her eyes.

"My pleasure." Kennin sat in the chair Jack had been sitting in. "Did you tell him about the drifting?"

Shinchou shook her head.

"Then how'd he know?" Kennin asked.

"I don't know," his sister said. She lifted her head as if she'd just thought of something. "That reminds me. You know that detective who came around here asking about that car you stole?"

"I didn't steal any car," Kennin said.

"Whatever. Anyway, he was here again today asking questions," Shinchou said.

"What kind of questions?" Kennin asked.

"Like where you were on this night or that night. Things like that."

"What'd you tell him?" Kennin asked.

"I told him to come back with a warrant if he wanted any answers," Shinchou said.

Kennin couldn't help smiling. "Thanks, sis."

The smile Shinchou returned was more crooked than straight. Her eyes grew watery, and new tears began to run down her cheeks. She hugged herself and trembled slightly. "What are we going to do?"

Kennin stared at the cigarette butts in the ashtray. Five thousand dollars was a lot of money, especially when a lowlife like Jack was looking for payback.

"I'll go talk to Dad," Kennin said.

13

The Nellis Minimum Security Prison Camp was located on the outskirts of Las Vegas. The convicts who were sent there were generally considered a low risk of escaping or of harming another inmate. In fact, according to Kennin's father, Mason, a lot of the inmates were people who would have been considered successful businessmen if they hadn't been caught breaking the law.

"Only ten bucks?" Mason Burnett grumbled the following afternoon. He was chewing on a Milky Way Kennin had just bought for him. Father and son were sitting at a picnic table in the visitor's area. Usually Kennin brought twenty dollars in quarters for his father's candy and snacks from the vending machine. But this week, with Shinchou not working, he'd only been able to bring ten.

"Money's tight, Dad," Kennin said. "Even the ten was hard to scrape up."

Mason grunted to show his dissatisfaction. Kennin knew from experience that it was best not to say anything more. He'd just have to wait until his father's mood passed.

The wait took a while. Mason was halfway through a bag of Skittles when he next spoke. "See that guy over there?"

Kennin slowly swiveled his head. "Which one?"

"Skinny little bald guy reading the book," his father said. "Guess how much he's worth?"

Kennin shrugged.

"Hundred million plus," Mason said.

"No way," Kennin said a shade too loudly.

"Keep it down," his father hissed. He pulled a smudged, folded piece of newspaper out of his pocket and slid it toward his son. There was no doubting that the photo accompanying the news story was of the skinny bald guy. According to this news clipping, he really had been worth more than a hundred million dollars before he'd been arrested for insider stock market trading.

"Amazing," Kennin said, handing the story back. "Only, what's insider trading?"

"It's when you buy or sell stock because you've gotten confidential information you're not supposed to have," Mason explained. "But here's what's really amazing. The guy's worth all that money, right? Guess how much he would have made on the illegal trades he got nailed for?"

"A couple of million?" Kennin guessed. After all, it would have been dumb to risk going to jail for less, wouldn't it?

"Two hundred thousand," his father said. "Can you believe it? Guy's worth a ton and he risks going to jail for peanuts."

"I don't get it," Kennin said.

"It's greed," his father said. "It's feeling like you'll never have enough. Believe me, if I had what he had, I'd probably be giving it away."

Kennin wasn't sure he believed that. He watched as his father gulped another handful of Skittles and drifted off in thought for a moment, no doubt imagining what life would be like with a hundred million dollars in the bank. Mason Burnett stretched his legs, which were too long for the sun-bleached khaki uniform that was standard issue for Nellis inmates. "So what's cookin' on the outside, Kennin?"

"Remember how I told you Shinchou was gonna start dancing so she could make better money?" Kennin asked. "Well, the guy who talked her into it also talked her into getting a boob job."

Kennin's father stopped chewing his candy bar. "And?"

"And now she's into him for five thousand plus the weekly vig," Kennin said.

Mason Burnett frowned and swore under his breath.

"He's pressuring her to start dancing, even though she isn't ready," Kennin said. "Like the vig is adding up every week and if she doesn't start soon, she'll never be able to pay him off."

"So why doesn't she dance?" his father asked.

"Because she's still recovering from the surgery," Kennin said. "I see her every day and I can tell she's still in a lot of pain. She's not faking it, Dad. If she could dance right now, she would."

Mason Burnett ran his fingers through his unkempt brown hair and nodded as if he was familiar with the scam. "You know this guy's name?"

"His first name's Jack and he has something to do with Rustler's Gentlemen's Club," Kennin said.

"I'll ask around and see what I can find out," Mason said. "I've made friends with some of the local guys in here. A couple of them are pretty heavy hitters. They might know who he is."

"It's not like we're trying to get out of paying the guy back," Kennin stressed. "Shinchou knows she has to make good on it. She just needs more time, that's all."

"I understand. I'll ask around. A lot'll depend on how well connected this Jack guy is. If he's in tight with the big boys, that could make him pretty much untouchable."

"Then what?" Kennin asked.

"Then you're on your own, kid," his father said.

The news was not reassuring. If Jack was well connected in the mob world of Vegas, then he and Shinchou were in trouble. "I understand, Dad, but if there's anything you can do, we'd really appreciate it."

"It'll take a couple of weeks, but I'll let you know."
Mason Burnett stood up. The visit was over.

Kennin also got up. "See you next week?"

"You bet," Mason said. "Just make sure you bring twenty
dollars' worth of quarters."

14

If there was one place that Kennin never expected to find himself, it was in the bleachers at a Dorado High football game. But there he was on a crisp, sunny fall afternoon, sitting in the noisy, crowded bleachers. In the distance, behind the opposing team's bleachers, a few of the taller mountain peaks wore small caps of white. Down on the field, the Dorado Dolphins were beating the Foothill Falcons 13–10.

Carrying a cardboard tray loaded with hot dogs and sodas, Tito climbed up through the crowded stands. "So when was the last time you went to a football game?" he asked loudly over the shouts and cheers of the crowd in the bleachers as he sat down beside Kennin.

"Not sure," Kennin said.

Tito slurped some soda through a straw. "How about this? You *ever* been to a football game?"

The answer was probably not. Nor was Kennin sure why he was at this one. He'd been on his way to the bus stop after school when Tito had grabbed him and insisted that they go. And this was the same Tito who'd refused to speak to Kennin for the past two weeks.

"Here you go, dude." Tito handed him a soda, then took a bite of his dog. "I mean, this is the life, right?" he said, his cheek bulging with food. "A beautiful day, fresh air, an exciting football game. This is what high school's all about."

Next to him, Kennin sat with the soda and hot dog still untouched in his lap. "I hope you won't mind me asking this, Tito, but what's going on?"

"What do you mean?" Tito asked through a mouthful of half-chewed hot dog and bun.

"I mean, you haven't talked to me for two weeks and now all of a sudden you drag me to this game and act like we're best friends again," Kennin said.

Tito took a gulp of soda and washed the food down. A roar went up from the crowd. Down on the field Chris Craven, in a blue and orange Dorado uniform, took the snap and faded back, looking for a receiver downfield. He found his man and launched a high, arching spiral. A gasp rose from the crowd as the receiver and a Foothill Falcons defender raced downfield. The Dorado receiver had beaten his man. If he caught the ball, there was no one between him and the end zone. In the bleachers people jumped to their feet. Kennin and Tito had no choice but to do the same if they wanted to see what happened.

"Ohhhh!" A collective groan of disappointment spread through the seats as the Dorado receiver reached for the ball, only to have it glance off his outstretched fingers and bounce out of bounds.

"Can you believe it?" Tito griped. "It was a perfect pass! Even I could have caught it."

Kennin had his doubts, but what interested him more was how Chris Craven stamped his foot in disgust. Moments later, when the dejected receiver returned to the huddle, Chris lit into him. Kennin couldn't hear what he was saying, but he could tell by the way the receiver hung his head that it wasn't exactly sweet talk.

The crowd sat down again and waited for the next play.

Tito looked at the untouched food in Kennin's lap. "You gonna eat that?"

Kennin picked up the dog and took a bite. It was lukewarm, and the bun tasted stale. But hey, it was a football game. Rah! Rah!

Tito leaned close to him. "Okay, look, I'm not angry anymore. This is my way of saying I forgive you for what happened. I mean, we're guys and I know we have certain urges. Even I have to admit that my sister's a pretty hot chick when she gets out of that garage and puts on makeup. But you did the right thing, *amigo.* Like I know Angelita's pretty upset and everything, but they say all's fair in love and war, right? I say, better to end it now before it gets serious than to wait until later."

Kennin took a sip of soda and said nothing. Maybe Tito had forgiven him, but he wasn't so sure he'd forgiven Tito. Meanwhile, a constant stream of people walked back and forth in front of the bleachers, visiting the concession stands or friends or whatever. Mariel Lewis and her crowd of followers passed. She looked up into the stands and caught Kennin's eye. For the past two weeks she'd given him a lot of looks. But she'd always kept her distance, and Kennin assumed that probably meant that she'd patched things up with Chris and didn't need to use other guys to get his attention anymore.

Mariel turned to her friends and said something. The next thing Kennin knew, they all swiveled their heads and looked up at him. The rest of the group moved on, but Mariel started to climb up through the crowded bleachers.

"Here comes trouble," Tito mumbled under his breath.

"Cool points, remember?" Kennin whispered back.

"Right, right, cool points," Tito repeated. "Easy for *you* to say. You've got the hottest babe in school climbing up the bleachers just to say hello."

Mariel reached their row and stood in front of them, put her hands on her hips, and cocked her head. "What you been up to, stranger?"

"Not much," Kennin said.

"Not getting up in time to make first-period math, huh?" Mariel said.

Kennin shrugged. He wasn't particularly proud of the fact that he missed the first period of school so often. But with Shinchou still recovering, there was a lot to do each morning. By the time he got up, and made sure his sister was set for the day, and caught the bus, it was often second or third period. He kept meaning to get up earlier, but it was hard to get going in the morning when he'd been at work until midnight.

Mariel went on talking and flirting with Kennin. What amazed Tito was that she could stand in front of them on the bleachers with the whole crowd watching and not appear the least bit self-conscious. As if she was absolutely certain of herself. Equally amazing was how, when Mariel decided she wanted to sit down next to Kennin, she merely looked at the sophomore on Kennin's right, giving the kid a silent message that it was time to slide over and fast. The sophomore moved so quickly he practically landed in the lap of the kid next to him.

Without missing a beat, Mariel sat down and continued chatting. It was all playful banter with teasing undertones. Tito had heard her try this with Kennin before. The difference was that in the past Kennin had kept his distance. This time he seemed more interested.

"I didn't think you were the type who came to football games," Mariel said.

"Once in a while," Kennin replied.

Tito made an involuntary gagging sound. Was this the same guy who fifteen minutes earlier had admitted that he wasn't sure he'd *ever* been to a game before? Kennin shot him a look that said *Chill out.*

Meanwhile, Mariel went right on with her playful banter. "You here to watch the game or are there other things you find more interesting?" It was a typical Mariel question.

"I think I enjoy the whole experience," Kennin answered.

"And you don't mind being up here in the bleachers?" Mariel asked.

"No," said Kennin. "Why would I?"

"Oh, I don't know." Mariel leaned toward him. "Personally, I like to get closer."

"You don't get to see as much," Kennin said.

"But when you're close you *feel* it more," Mariel cooed.

Tito stifled a groan.

"I never thought about that," Kennin said.

"You definitely should," said Mariel.

A shout rose from the crowd. Down on the field Chris faked a handoff, then scrambled out around the weak side. The noise increased, and fans started to rise in the bleachers as Chris broke one tackle and then another. With each broken tackle the crowd cheered and shouted louder and louder, but Mariel hardly seemed to notice. Her focus was entirely on Kennin.

"Oh, yeah!" Even Tito couldn't restrain from cheering

as Chris broke the last tackle and charged into the end zone for a touchdown, spiking the ball and then dropping to one knee.

At that point, Mariel turned to look. Not because of what had happened, but as if she was annoyed that the roar of the crowd was interfering with her conversation with Kennin. Tito couldn't believe it. Down on the field Mariel's boyfriend had just scored a touchdown. But Mariel couldn't have cared less.

Meanwhile, Kennin appeared more amused than anything else. "You don't care when your boyfriend scores?"

"Him?" Mariel said, as if she was completely bored. "He scores all the time."

In the end zone, the Dorados crowded around Chris, slapping his shoulder pads and patting his helmet, congratulating the quarterback on his touchdown. Tito watched as Chris pulled off his helmet. Despite the cool, dry fall air, his hair glistened with sweat and was plastered against his forehead. He had a grin on his lips, but then his gaze began to rise upward toward the bleachers. Tito realized that he was looking for Mariel. The expression on Chris's face changed. Mariel had turned her face toward Kennin and appeared to be whispering something in his ear. Down on the field Chris's face hardened. His eyes narrowed with anger, and then he looked away.

15

Angelita couldn't believe her brother. "You told him *what*?"

"I said you'd drive us up to the new course and maybe let him take a test run," Tito said.

Sitting at her desk in her bedroom, Angelita looked up from the computer where she'd been working on her college essay. The idea of being in the car with Kennin sent her into a turmoil. He'd completely ignored her since the night she'd spent at his place. She was hurt and angry, and was basically doing her best to forget he'd ever existed. And now her brother was trying to undo all that work. No sooner did he suggest they drive up to see the new run than she could feel that tiny flower of hope she'd been trying to kill off spring back to life. It grew out of that soft, fertile part of her that still clung to the thinnest hope that somehow she'd misread him. The part of her that whispered that perhaps this was just his way, and she simply had to be patient and wait. Meanwhile, the rest of her screamed that she was an idiot and a fool to think that, and that she was deluding herself.

"Why should I take him anywhere?" Angelita asked.

"Because it's a new course he's never run before, and if he doesn't get some seat time it's gonna be really hard for him to win," Tito said.

"So?"

"So I've still got every penny I own riding on this tsuiso, and if Kennin loses I am completely and totally screwed, broke, and trashed."

Angelita gave him a *Why should I care?* look and turned back to her computer. As soon as she finished this essay she would mail out the application to the University of California. Next would follow the slow, tedious, stressful wait for an answer—the letter that she prayed would begin with the words, "Congratulations, you have been accepted . . ." Then she'd know for certain that her new life was beginning. A life far away from her overprotective mother and goofy brother, and far away from the sleaze of Las Vegas, and most definitely a life that would no longer include Kennin Burnett.

"You want to know why you should care?" Tito sputtered, bringing her back to the present. "Because I'm your brother, okay? Because we're family, and family is supposed to help each other through tough times."

Angelita was tempted to ask where Tito had been during her tough times—all those nights these past two weeks
when she'd cried herself to sleep, and the mornings when
the dread of seeing Kennin in school made it almost impossible for her to get out of bed. But that wasn't fair, because
Tito hadn't known about that. She'd kept it a secret.

"So?" Tito said.

"So . . . what?" asked Angelita.

"You'll do it, right?" he said. "You'll take us up there?"

"I'll think about it." Angelita started to type again,
aware that her brother was still hovering over her. She
looked up and glared at him. "Would you mind? I'd like
some privacy."

"But I need to know," Tito said.

"And I said I'd think about it, okay?"

"Well, can you think about it fast?" her brother asked.

"Why?" Angelita asked. But no sooner had the question
left her lips than she realized exactly why. The realization
was like a heavy weight descending onto her shoulders. It
filled her with renewed fury at her brother. "Don't you dare
tell me he's on his way here right now?"

"Well, yeah," Tito admitted sheepishly. "Like, he should
be here any second."

If Angelita had been annoyed before, she was completely furious now. Her brother had the most unbelievable
nerve! Without asking her, he'd told Kennin that she'd drive

them. But what was even more infuriating was the part of her that was actually _glad_ her brother had done it. That part of her that had previously said to wait and be patient, and was now telling her to hurry up and change into nicer clothes, put on makeup, and fix her hair.

She felt the fury drain out of her, replaced by that ridiculously feeble, needy dream of romance. As if Kennin was her prince. It was such a stupid, immature fantasy, and yet once again she knew she was going to fall for it. Because that part of her always won. She should have told her brother and Kennin to go to hell, but she never would. She just wasn't that kind of girl. So instead she did what she always did. She let out a big sigh and said, "All right, give me a few minutes."

"You're the best," Tito said. "Really, you won't be sorry."

A wave of bitterness swept through her and she was tempted to say something rude, but as always she held her tongue. As soon as Tito left, she hurried into the bathroom to wash up and think about what she would wear. She hated herself for doing it, but she couldn't help herself either. All she could think about was the way Mariel Lewis dressed. Should she dare wear something tight and low cut? That was so unlike her. Was she really that desperate? No. She would dress nice for Kennin, but not like a slut. After all, if Kennin wanted a slut, he already knew where to find one.

She had just finished brushing her hair when she heard Tito call from the hall. "Kennin's here."

She went downstairs and found them sitting at the kitchen table. Mrs. Rivera was setting out a plate of plantains for them.

"Go ahead, eat," she was saying to Kennin, as if she'd known him for years. "You look too thin."

With a start, Angelita realized her mother was right. Kennin did look thinner than she remembered. She'd spent so much time these past two weeks avoiding him that she hadn't noticed. She watched as he took a bite of a plantain and chewed it slowly. She could tell that he was hungry but too polite to wolf the food down.

"Hi," Angelita said.

Kennin smiled at her. "Hey."

There was something warm and sincere about his greeting that disconcerted her. Unless one of them was crazy, she was certain it wasn't the smile of a player who used girls and tossed them aside.

"Angelita, this is Tito's friend Kennin," her mother said. "You know, the one he's always talking about. You can see he's a very nice boy."

Mrs. Rivera was big on first impressions. Angelita wondered what her mother would say if she knew he was the one she'd spent the night with a few weeks before.

Mrs. Rivera was still hovering over them. "Maybe your

friend would like something to drink, Tito. Angelita, ask Tito's friend if he'd like something to drink."

Angelita had been through this scene too many times before to bother asking her mother why she couldn't ask him herself. Instead she said, "Would you like something to drink?"

"Have any milk?" Kennin asked.

The request caught Angelita by surprise. It was so . . . wholesome. She went to the refrigerator, got the milk, and poured him a glass.

"Thanks," he said when she placed it on the table in front of him. Again, there was something sincere about him. It just didn't make sense to her. How could this be the same boy who'd blown her off so coldly for the past few weeks?

They finished eating. Kennin politely thanked Mrs. Rivera for the food. Then they went out to the garage. This time, when they got into the car, Tito sat in the front while Kennin folded himself into the back. There was more room since they weren't carrying the extra tires, but it was still uncomfortable without a seat. They drove down the Las Vegas strip, passing the imitation of the Empire State Building and the Statue of Liberty at the New York, New York Casino, and the imitation Eiffel Tower at the Paris. It was late afternoon, and slanting orange sunlight glared off the windows of the buildings, giving the downtown a fiery look. Sometimes it seemed to Kennin that nothing about Las Vegas was real.

As they headed out of town and into the desert, Tito recited the directions from a piece of paper he'd pulled out of his pocket. "We stay on this road for about five miles. I'll tell you when to turn."

In the back, Kennin was silent. Angelita assumed he was looking at the barren landscape of brush, rock, and cactus. But once, when she looked at him in the rearview mirror, she found him looking right back at her. Was that longing in his eyes, or was it just her overly hopeful imagination?

"Why run in a new place?" Angelita asked, more to cut through the silence than because she wanted to know the answer.

"Chris says the cops are less likely to look for us here," her brother answered. "It's more out of the way."

He was right about that, Angelita thought. They were surrounded by barren high desert, reddish outcroppings of rock, and dry brown brush.

"Hey, here's the turnoff," Tito said.

Angelita turned onto a side road. In the back, Kennin immediately sensed that the asphalt was rough and uneven. Not exactly prime drifting surface. The car started to climb uphill through a winding turn. The road seemed awfully narrow for drifting.

"How're two cars gonna drift through here?" Tito asked.

"I'm not even sure how one car is going to do it," Kennin said.

A little farther up they passed a yellow triangular sign:

NARROW ROAD
USE CAUTION
YIELD TO
DOWNHILL TRAFFIC

"I can't say that contributes to a feeling of confidence," Tito quipped.

They entered the bottom of a set of S-turns curling through a winding ravine with walls of solid reddish rock on either side. There was no room for error here, only about two feet of rough gravel between the edge of the pavement and the base of the rock walls.

"Carajo!" Tito exclaimed. "This is a death trap!"

The road got steeper and the turns sharper until it became a series of switchbacks.

"How do we know where the start is?" Tito wondered out loud.

The answer was just around the bend, where half a dozen cars were parked along the side of the road. Kennin recognized Ian's white Cressida, Chris's Jeep Cherokee with the dinged front fender from the party at Mariel's the month before, Megs's light blue Toyota Corolla with metallic silver racing stripes, and Driftdog's singed and dented SX 180 hatchback. The car now sported a light green front quarter panel—hardly a match for the rest of the body, which was mostly blackened, scorched red paint. The guys were standing in a small group on the roadside, watching as Angelita's 240 SX came around the bend.

"Man, I can't believe Driftdog got that thing running again," Tito said while Angelita pulled up behind the SX 180. "It's like the car with nine lives."

They got out of the 240 SX. It was at least ten degrees cooler up here than in downtown Las Vegas, and a stiff breeze across the hilltops added to the chill. There was nothing except the road, gravel, brush, and scattered boulders. Angelita hugged herself as she and the others walked toward the group of drivers. Kennin wasn't surprised to see Ian's lips moving, probably muttering some racist epithet under his breath.

Driftdog Dave left the others and came toward them, offering Kennin his hand. Ever since Kennin had pulled him from his burning car, Driftdog had been the friendliest driver in the group.

"Hey, man, how's it going?" Driftdog asked.

"Not bad. See you got your ride up and running again," Kennin said.

Driftdog smiled proudly. "As long as there's junkyards and eBay, they can't keep old Driftdog down." But just as quickly the smile passed and he dropped his voice. "Man, you believe they want to run here? It's frickin' suicide."

By now they'd reached the rest of the group. Megs

greeted them. Ian and Chris nodded silently. Ever since that visit Mariel had paid to Kennin in the bleachers during the football game, Chris had taken to giving him ominous looks.

"So what do you think?" Megs asked, obviously referring to the course.

"I think there's a good chance someone's gonna get hurt," Kennin said.

"There's no place else left," Chris said. "The cops have really turned up the heat. They're randomly patrolling all the other spots at night. I don't know about the rest of you guys, but I'm really tired of starting tsuisos and seeing them busted up before we can finish."

"Why don't we all just agree we can't do it and forget the bets?" Tito suggested.

"The hell with that," Ian scoffed, and gestured at Kennin. "You bet your man here could kick our butts. I for one don't buy it, 'cause all I've seen so far is a no-drift wuss."

Kennin fought the urge to ball his hands into fists, knowing that was precisely what Ian wanted.

"Do me a favor, Ian," Megs said. "Let's see if we can have just one frickin' conversation without you trying to pick a fight, okay? Now, it's real simple. There are five of us here. I happen to know that the other three will go along with whatever we decide. So it's a question of, do we run or not?"

"I say we run," said Ian.

"I say forget it," said Driftdog Dave.

That left Chris, Megs, and Kennin.

"There's another option," Angelita interrupted. "You could run legitimate. I bet we could get the raceway to let us use their parking lot. We could set out a course with cones. That's what they do in a lot of places."

"Places that don't have mountains," Ian said. "True drifting's a mountain sport. That crap they do in parking lots is for wimps."

Kennin thought it was interesting that Ian, the least experienced drifter in the group, would say that.

"Well, it may be for wimps, but I have to agree with Angelita that it's probably a better idea than running here," Megs said. "It's too steep and narrow. And those frickin' S-turns down that ravine are freaky. I say forget this. Wait till the cops get tired of patrolling the old spots. Sooner or later they'll find something else to do. Then we'll go back and run there."

That made it two to one in favor of not running the tsuiso. Everyone's eyes turned to Chris and Kennin.

"I say run," Chris said. "It's a fair comp. We'll all be at the same disadvantage."

Now it was even: two to run, two against it. Everyone turned to Kennin.

"How about it, champ?" Ian sneered. "You got balls or no balls?"

16

Instead of answering, Kennin turned to Angelita. "Let's go talk."

"What, you gotta get permission?" Ian taunted.

"Shut up, Ian," Megs said. "It's her car."

Kennin led Angelita a dozen yards away. The orange sun was dropping over the distant peaks to the west, and down in the Great Basin, long shadows were slowly engulfing the city of Las Vegas. Angelita was certain Kennin wanted to ask her how she felt about his using her car on such a dangerous run. But what she was thinking was far from what she was feeling. She couldn't understand why he was being so sincere and nice. How could this be the same guy who'd ignored her for the past two weeks? Was there something she'd missed?

Kennin turned and engulfed her with his dark eyes. She felt a tremble inside. There was something about his intense seriousness that was magnetic. "Megs said what I was going to say," he said. "It's your car."

Angelita knew what the rational answer should have been: It was far too risky. She'd spent months working on the 240 SX, not to mention a significant amount of money. Had anyone else asked her, the answer would have been no. Even with Kennin, her answer *should* have been no. But no matter what logic said, her heart wouldn't let her say it to him. "How bad do you want to drive?"

Kennin looked down at the cracked asphalt and shrugged. "I don't care that much." But then he looked up and his eyes met hers. "But if I do drive, I drive to win."

Angelita understood what he meant. With winning came risks. She'd seen the course. It wasn't like before, where Kennin could lag behind until the wide last turn and then slip ahead. Running this course would be a battle from start to finish. And few knights ever returned from battle unharmed. He was waiting for her answer.

"If you don't drive, you'll never hear the end of it," she said.

Kennin gave her an astonished look. As if that was the last answer he'd expected. He put his hand on her arm and stared intently into her eyes. Angelita sensed a yearning radiating from him. It reminded her of the night she'd stayed at his place. Her heart began to lift. So he still felt it! She was almost certain that if those other guys hadn't been there, he would have taken her in his arms and kissed her. Instead he glanced back at them, and at Tito in particular. Angelita was instantly puzzled. Why was Kennin looking at her brother? Could he possibly have anything to do with this?

Instead of kissing her, Kennin merely squeezed her arm and thanked her. Then he started to turn away, as if to rejoin the group. But she grabbed his arm. "Wait."

He turned and held her with his eyes.

"What were the past two weeks about?" she asked.

His eyes told her he knew what she was asking, but he was unable to give her the true answer. Instead, he averted his glance. Suddenly Angelita knew that it hadn't been his decision to avoid her. There'd been some other reason. Something she didn't know about.

Meanwhile, Kennin turned back to the group. "I'll drive here," he said.

There was a moment of silence. The small group of drivers exchanged looks. The final decision had been made. It was three to two in favor of running the tsuiso.

"All right," Chris said. "The tsuiso is on. We run tomorrow night. Here."

"How about some practice runs first?" Driftdog asked.

"When?" Megs asked.

"Right now."

"What? In my Jeep?" Chris asked. "What good is that?"

"At least you can get familiar with the course," Megs said.

Chris didn't look happy. "Okay, two runs each just to learn the course."

The others agreed and returned to their cars. Tito started to reach for the 240 SX's door, but Kennin whispered, "Don't get in."

Tito stopped and frowned. "Why not?"

"I want to be the last," Kennin said.

"So what do you want us to do instead?" Tito asked.

"I don't know," Kennin said. "Wait, enjoy the sunset, whatever."

"The sun just set," Tito pointed out.

Angelita groaned. "Try not to be so literal, okay?"

By now the other guys had gotten into their cars and started their engines. One by one they headed down the course, while Angelita, Tito, and Kennin stood beside the 240 SX pretending to talk.

"Nice clouds, huh?" Tito joked. A few minutes before, the clouds had been a deep purple edged with bright pink. But now they were quickly fading into the night.

Neither Angelita nor Kennin responded. Had her brother not been there, Angelita had a feeling the conversation would have been entirely different. Finally, when the other cars had gone, they got into the 240 SX and headed down the course. Kennin drove carefully, studying each curve.

"So, what do you think?" Tito asked from the backseat as they wound down through the switchbacks.

"It's gonna be tight," Kennin said. "And it's not like there's a lot of shoulder to use."

The switchbacks ended and they approached a familiar-looking yellow sign:

NARROW ROAD

USE CAUTION

YIELD TO

UPHILL TRAFFIC

"On the way up it said yield to downhill traffic," Tito said.

"And this is why," Angelita said as they entered the S-turns that dropped through the narrow walls of jagged rock.

"Dude, I'm freaked just driving through here and not drifting," Tito said, looking up through the windows at the tall walls of reddish brown rock on either side. "I frickin' can't imagine what it's gonna be like in a battle."

"I hate to remind you of this, dear brother," Angelita said, "but you're the one who wants him to run so bad."

"Yeah, but I'm just saying," Tito started to say, then stopped. "Aw, forget it."

They got to the bottom of the run, where the other cars were waiting. Then they all drove back up and headed down again. By now it was dark, and a sliver of moon was rising. Once again Kennin went last. Only this time, when they got to the S-turns, he pulled the car to the side of the road. In the shadows of the ravine it was almost pitch black.

"What's going on?" Tito asked.

"I want to take a closer look," Kennin said, and turned to Angelita. "You have a flashlight?"

"After that fire with Driftdog, I'll never leave home without one," she said, taking a long black flashlight out of the glove compartment.

They got out, and Kennin shined the light at the road and walls of rock. The course narrowed in this spot to the point where it did not seem possible for two cars to fit. The rocky walls on either side were rough and scarred with deep gashes and different colors of paint where cars and trucks had scraped against them in the past.

"You meet a car coming in the other direction here, it's an instant head-on," Tito said.

"Megs and Mutt'll make sure the road's clear," Kennin said and peered down the road through the ravine. "What would you say is the narrowest spot?"

"Let's see." Tito walked down the road. Unlike man-made ravines where road engineers used explosives to blast a chasm through solid rock, this gorge was natural. It appeared the engineers had decided it was just wide enough on its own. The question in Kennin's mind was, wide enough for what?

"Here." Tito stopped. "I think this is probably the narrowest."

"How wide do you think it is?" Kennin asked.

"Give me a second." Tito started to walk across the road, heel to toe.

"Trying to figure if there's room for two cars?" Angelita asked Kennin in the dark.

"Guess it'll depend on which two cars," Kennin said.

"Thirteen, fourteen feet," Tito said.

"Wider than it looks," Kennin said.

"So it's an optical illusion," Angelita said. "It looks narrower than it really is because the walls beside it are so tall."

"My sister, the brain," said Tito, and looked at Kennin. "Anything else you want to see?"

"No, that's it," Kennin said. "Let's go home."

With Angelita driving, they rode silently back toward the bright lights of Las Vegas. The route took them down Las Vegas Avenue, past the Babylon Casino and the erupting volcano in front of the Mirage. A few blocks later they passed Rustler's Gentlemen's Club, the place where Jack the jackass hung out and where Shinchou worked. Kennin's sister had finally felt well enough to go back to work, and since then their schedules had been so different that she and Kennin hardly saw each other. Parked on the street outside the club was Jack the jackass's yellow 'vette. Jack was standing beside it, talking to a girl whose straight blond hair had hot pink streaks. She was wearing a tight red tube top, tiny white shorts, and high white boots.

As Kennin watched, Jack put his hands on the blonde's hips and pulled her close. She was gazing up at him with an excited expression, and he spoke softly with a knowing smile. Kennin couldn't hear what they were saying, but he watched her nod eagerly and then stretch up on her toes to kiss him on the lips. It was a long kiss, and more than a friendly one. Kennin knew he shouldn't have been surprised.

"What are you looking at?" Tito asked.

"Nothing," Kennin said, looking ahead again.

"Yeah, right, Mr. Mysterious," Tito said doubtfully.

Now that they were downtown, Angelita glanced over at Kennin. "Drop you somewhere?"

Kennin looked back at her and didn't answer. Maybe it was her imagination, but once again it seemed like he would have said something were Tito not there. Finally he pointed ahead. "A couple of corners up would be great."

"We could drop you off at home if you like," Tito said.

"It's okay," Kennin said. "I mean, it's pretty far out of the way."

"Hey, not a problem," Tito said. "It's still early. Not like I'm in a rush to go anywhere else."

It was obvious that Tito was curious to see where Kennin lived, and it was hard for Kennin to argue that it was better to pay for a bus than accept a free ride.

It was up to Angelita to save him. "I really should get home," she said. "I still have a lot of homework to do."

"Typical," Tito muttered as his sister pulled over to the curb.

Meanwhile, in the front, Kennin glanced at Angelita and silently mouthed the word "Thanks." Then he opened the door and got out. Tito got out with him.

"So tomorrow night, man," Tito said, slapping Kennin's palm. "We'll set 'em up, shut 'em down, take the money and run, right?"

"Right," Kennin said.

"Catch you in school tomorrow?"

"Definitely," Kennin said.

Tito got into the front, and Angelita pulled the Nissan back into traffic. In the rearview mirror she watched Kennin start to cross the dark street and then disappear into the night.

"Strange guy, huh?" Tito said in the seat next to her.

"What do you mean?" Angelita asked.

"Well, you know. It's like he doesn't want us to know anything about him: where he lives and what his family's like, stuff like that."

It was obvious that Tito wasn't thinking clearly, or he would have remembered the night she had not come home. Did he think she and Kennin spent it in a motel?

"I just think you gotta be careful with a guy like that,"

Tito said. "I know he's my friend and everything, but I wouldn't get too close, know what I mean?"

"Tito, did you say something to him?" Angelita asked.

"About what?"

"After that night I didn't come home," she said.

"What do you mean?" her brother asked.

"Something happened after that night. He changed completely. It was like night and day."

"Hey, you know how guys are," her brother said. "They get what they want and they're out of there."

"How do you know he got what he wanted?" Angelita asked. "Did he say something?"

"No, but come on," Tito said. "You spent the night."

"So?" Angelita said. "You don't know what happened. And maybe you haven't noticed, but he isn't exactly acting like a guy who's out of there either."

"Like I said, he's hard to figure out," Tito said. "That's why it's best not to get too close."

"You still haven't answered my question," Angelita said. "Did you say something to him or not?"

"Like what?" Tito asked.

"I don't know, Tito. Something that would turn him off or make him stay away."

Tito was quiet for a moment. Then he said, "No, I never said anything like that to him."

17

Kennin caught a bus home. When he got there, the trailer was filled with sweet-smelling smoke. Shinchou was reclining on the couch in her bathrobe, her eyes closed, thin white wires from an iPod snaking into earphones in her ears. As Kennin stepped quietly in, he wondered where she'd gotten it. He didn't have to wonder what the sweet smell was. The answer lay in a plastic Baggie on the table next to the ashtray. He walked into the kitchenette. His sister's eyes were still closed, and it was difficult to tell if she even knew he was there. He opened the refrigerator expecting the usual meager selection, and was surprised to find the shelves stocked with fruit, sliced meat, cheese, and bread.

He chose an apple—it had been a while since he'd had one—and closed the refrigerator. At the sound of the door closing, Shinchou opened her eyes. She blinked and looked for a moment as if she wasn't sure where she was. Kennin rinsed the apple under the tap.

"Thanks for getting all this food," Kennin said.

Shinchou nodded slowly. In fact, everything about her appeared to be moving in slow motion.

"Where'd you get the iPod?" Kennin asked.

"At the Apple Store," Shinchou answered.

"Which model?"

"Forty gigs."

Kennin felt his eyebrows rise. He was pretty sure that was one of the most expensive. He knew she was working at the club, but he was under the impression that any extra money she earned was supposed to go to Jack to pay off the five grand. Clearly some of the money Shinchou made was going toward other things, not to mention the source of the sweet-smelling smoke.

As if she'd read his mind, Shinchou said, "Jack doesn't have to know about every penny I earn."

"But what about the vig?" Kennin asked.

"Screw the vig and screw you." Shinchou bristled. "You're not the one grinding your butt up on that stage while gross old men stare and try to grab you when the manager isn't looking. As long as I'm working my ass off, Jack's getting what he wants, maybe not as fast as he wants it, but that's too bad. If he has to wait a little longer for his money, that's tough luck."

There was an unexpected knock on the trailer door.

Shinchou straightened up, suddenly alert. "You expecting someone?"

Kennin shook his head.

Shinchou reached toward the glass ashtray and quickly removed certain incriminating pieces of evidence, including the plastic bag, which she hid under a pillow on the couch. Meanwhile, Kennin went to the door and peeked out, but all he could see was the top of a head. Whoever was out there was on the short side. He glanced back at his sister and shrugged his shoulder to indicate that he couldn't tell who it was. By now Shinchou had hidden everything. She nodded back that it was okay to open the door.

"Who is it?" Kennin asked.

"Derek Jamison," came the answer.

Kennin rolled his eyes as if telling Shinchou not to worry. Then he opened the door and stepped out into the dark. Parked next to the trailer was a massive black Hummer with huge custom rims and an enormous chrome grill that made the front end look like some kind of square comic-book monster.

As Kennin closed the trailer door behind him, Derek took a deep sniff and exhaled with a grin. "Hey, how come I wasn't invited to the party?"

Kennin ignored that. "What's up?"

Derek looked around the trailer park. "Nice digs, kid."

"You come all this way to tell me that?" Kennin asked.

"It's not like you got a phone number," Derek said.

"You can always find me at the Babylon," Kennin said.

"I just wanted to check you out firsthand," Derek said, staring past him at the trailer again.

Kennin wasn't sure what Derek meant by that, but he had a feeling he'd find out soon enough.

"So you know the drifting promotion we talked about the other day at the casino?" Derek said. "Mr. Mercado has decided he wants to go ahead with it."

"Good," Kennin said.

"We're gonna have a Babylon Casino drifting team," Derek said. "Mr. Mercado wants you to be on it. It'll be a good thing, kid. You and your friends can get off the street and start drifting legit. It'll be a lot safer, and in the long run you'll make better money."

Kennin nodded silently. There was no point in telling Mercado's wingman that if he was going to drift, he preferred the street, and that he wished there was no money involved.

Derek took a white envelope from his jacket pocket and handed it to Kennin.

"What's this?" Kennin asked.

"An agreement," Derek answered. "Terms for being on the drift team. Read it over, but don't wait too long. Mr. Mercado wants to get going on this pretty fast."

Kennin slid the envelope into his back pocket. "Thanks."

"One other thing," Derek said. "A little birdie told me

you and your friends might be planning one of those drift races up in the mountains tomorrow night. If I were you, I'd skip it."

Kennin didn't react. He had to make sure not to reveal his surprise that Derek knew about the tsuiso the next night. The whole thing had only been decided a couple of hours ago. How could Derek possibly have found out about it? At the same time, Derek studied him closely and broke into an unexpected smile. "You're good, kid, real good. You'd make a fair card player, you know that?"

"If you say so," Kennin said, and went back into the trailer.

18

Shinchou didn't go to work that night. Kennin asked if she had the night off and she told him to mind his own business.

In the morning he got up early and headed for school. For once he was determined to make it in time for first-period math. Fall in Nevada was beautiful. The air was clear and crisp and there were more birds in the trees than during the scalding heat of the summer. Ironically, the casinos, which were Las Vegas's main attraction, had no windows. Casino owners like Mike Mercado didn't want gamblers to be distracted by anything happening outside. They wanted gamblers to focus on gambling and nothing else.

Kennin was walking to the bus stop when he became aware of a black Escalade rolling slowly along the street beside him. The car had twenty-inch custom rims and black

windows. Kennin couldn't see in, but he had a feeling that whoever was inside was watching him.

The back passenger windows went down and Jack the jackass poked his head out. "Hey, looky looky."

Kennin kept walking. The Escalade rolled alongside.

"What's the matter, boy? Don't feel like talking?" Jack asked.

Kennin stopped on the sidewalk and faced the car, which also stopped. "How can I help you, Jack?"

"Where're you going?" Jack asked. "Maybe we can give you a ride."

"Thanks, but I prefer to walk," said Kennin.

The smile disappeared from Jack's face. "Maybe you want to get in the car anyway."

"Maybe I don't," Kennin answered.

Jack turned and said something to someone in the Escalade who Kennin couldn't see. The front passenger door opened, and a guy the size of a sumo wrestler got out. He had a shaved head and was wearing dark shades, a black sweatshirt, sweatpants, and heavy black boots. A thick silver chain with a medallion hung around his neck. Kennin was pretty sure he could outrun the goon, but that wasn't the point. He wasn't about to give Jack the jackass or his friends the pleasure of seeing him run.

"Get in the car," the goon said. The rear passenger door swung open and Jack slid over to make room. Kennin got in. The Escalade reeked of cigarette smoke. The goon rode shotgun and Kennin sat behind him. The guy had to have the fattest neck he'd ever seen, and dead center was a small red tattoo of a heart. The driver—Kennin only saw the greasy black hair at the back of his head—put the Escalade in gear and pulled away from the curb. Inside, Jack lit a cigarette and offered one to Kennin.

"No, thanks," Kennin said.

"Your sister's the only one in the family who smokes?" Jack said.

"No, our father smokes too," said Kennin.

"Father? Shinchou never told me she had a father," said Jack.

"You thought we were immaculately conceived?" Kennin asked.

The greasy-haired driver chuckled, but Jack frowned, clearly not amused. "So what's his story?"

"He's around," was all Kennin cared to say. The Escalade was in traffic now. Kennin wondered where they were going. "You know, I was on my way someplace."

"You'll get there," Jack said. "Sooner or later."

Kennin settled back into the Escalade's leather seat. Guess he'd have to wait until tomorrow to make it to first-period math. They drove. Jack smoked and said nothing, no doubt hoping the silence would make Kennin anxious. After a while Kennin realized they were heading away from downtown.

"So listen, boy," Jack finally said. "I got a problem with your sister."

"Then why don't you talk to her?" Kennin asked.

"I have," Jack said. "Believe me, I've talked till I was blue in the face. But you know how women are. They don't listen to reason. I don't think your sister really understands the way business works around here. A man pays for something, he expects results. People don't give away five grand for no reason. This ain't the Shinchou Charity here, boy. You know that."

Kennin didn't bother to answer.

"Now, your sister, she seems to think she can get something for nothing, understand?" Jack went on. "I laid out a lot of money for her and she ain't exactly been considerate about paying me back."

"You never told me how much the vig was," Kennin asked.

Jack blinked as if the question had caught him off guard. "Same as it is for everyone else. Five percent. In your sister's case, that would be two hundred and fifty a week."

In the world of bank loans and credit cards, interest was paid monthly. Only in the world of loan sharks was the interest paid weekly. A 5 percent vig on $5,000 meant that Shinchou was expected to come up with $250 a week in addition to the $5,000 she had to pay back. The whole idea was to make the borrower take forever to pay back the loan, but in the meantime fork over $250 a week, week after week, month after month, year after year. No wonder a jerk like Jack could afford to drive around in a brand-new 'vette.

"Now the problem is, not only has your sister been slow paying the vig," Jack went on, "but she don't always show up for work when she's supposed to. Like last night she was a no-show. And when she does show up, she's got a real bad attitude. And the customers don't like that."

Kennin knew what was coming, but he waited to hear it from Jack anyway.

"Normally," Jack continued, "we got ways of dealing with people who got bad attitudes and who get behind on the vig. Tiny, here, he's real good at getting people back in line."

The giant goon in the front seat turned and grinned. The gold in his teeth clashed with the silver necklace.

"But your sister is a special problem," Jack explained. "See, in my business, she's the merchandise the customers come to see. So it don't do me no good to have damaged merchandise, because then the customers don't want to pay to see her. It's like, like . . ."

"Like biting yourself in the ass," said the greasy-haired driver.

"Right," said Jack. "So I gotta find other means of persuasion, you understand, boy?"

Kennin nodded. He began understanding about five minutes ago.

"Now you tell me," Jack said. "What do *you* think I can do to get your sister to cooperate and show up for work and pay back the money she owes?"

Kennin looked out the window just as the Escalade turned past a chain-link gate and drove into what looked like a deserted construction site. Suddenly he understood why Jack had taken so long to get to his point. He was waiting until they reached their destination.

19

Inside the construction site, the Escalade bounced through dirt potholes and over planks of wood. It was apparent from the piles of broken concrete, brick, and rubble that some old buildings had been torn down to make way for a new, larger building. The Escalade stopped behind a large pile of rubble, out of sight from the street and sidewalk. Inside the car, Jack gazed at Kennin. "I'm still waiting for your answer. What do I got to do to get your sister to cooperate?"

Kennin stared back at him and didn't say anything.

Jack frowned. "Boy, I don't think you understand the fix you're in."

"You think if you beat the crap out of me that'll somehow get my sister to pay you on time?" Kennin asked.

Jack grinned. "Why, I am amazed that you would imagine such a thing. Me, resort to physical violence? What good would it do me to kick the crap out of you? Would that increase the balance in my bank account? No, of course it wouldn't. Sorry, boy, but you disappoint me. I guess I was right when I said you truly do not understand how things work around here. Let me explain it a bit more clearly. When we picked you up before, you were on your way to school. And after school you were planning to go to your little mechanic girlfriend's place and you and she and that dill-weed brother of hers were gonna head up into the mountains. Am I right?"

Kennin didn't answer. There was no point in affirming or denying it. The thing he couldn't understand was how Jack could have *known* about it. How did some small-time hood who ran a strip joint know what was going on in a high school? It was like last night at the trailer. How had Derek known about it?

Jack grinned. "Not bad, boy. That's a pretty good poker face for a kid your age. You ever think about trying your hand at cards? You might have a talent there."

Funny, that was exactly what Derek had said the night before. Still, Kennin waited.

"Okay, boy, so here's the score," Jack said. "I can do your sister a favor. Take a little heat off her, so to speak."

He paused as if he thought Kennin should understand what he was getting at. But the truth was, Kennin did not understand. At least, not yet.

"Boy, I don't know if you're aware of this, but you are

the odds-on favorite to win this little street-racing event tonight," Jack said. "Now, you know this is a gambling town, and there's folks who'll bet on anything, including how long it takes spit to dry on the sidewalk."

Now Kennin knew what Jack wanted. "You want me to tank?"

"You catch on quick, boy," Jack said. "Yeah, that's exactly what you're gonna do. Not the first heat, although if that's how it goes down, so be it. But I think the second heat's the one where you're gonna lose."

"And what does my sister get in return?"

"I just might be a little more understanding the next time she don't show up for work or don't pay the vig on time," Jack said.

Kennin gazed out the Escalade's window. Not that there was much to see. Just the rubble and the tall plywood fence that surrounded the site and blocked the public's view. Then he turned back to Jack. "I'll think about it."

He reached for the door, but there was a loud *click*. Greasy Hair in the front seat had activated the child-safety locks.

"Sorry, boy, but just *thinking* about it won't do," Jack said. "There's gonna be too much riding on this event to depend on some little snot *thinking* about it, understand?"

As if there was any doubt, Tiny turned slightly in the

front seat and swiveled his massive bald head until his eyes met Kennin's.

"You've got me locked in a car in the back of a construction site with two thugs," Kennin replied calmly. "Am I really supposed to believe I have a choice?"

Jack grinned. "No, I guess you ain't."

20

That morning Angelita waited for Kennin near the city bus stop. She wanted to talk to him. She wanted to find out if the reason he'd been so distant was because of something Tito might have said. When first period started and Kennin did not arrive, she continued to wait, even though it meant that she'd miss class, something she hated to do.

Every ten minutes another Citizen Area Transit bus would arrive, and Angelita's hopes would rise, only to fall when the doors opened and Kennin wasn't there. As second period approached, she felt herself growing anxious. She might allow herself to skip one class this morning, but she couldn't skip two, not without risking a call to her mother from the attendance office. Finally she hurried back to school.

That left only one other option. She would have to talk

to him at lunch. Angelita hated that idea. Everyone in the cafeteria would see them. Tongues would wag as gossip filled the air. But what choice did she have?

As fifth period approached, Angelita felt her anxiety increase. She kept reminding herself that she didn't *have* to speak to him. No one was forcing her to. But it *felt* as if she had no choice.

The bell rang, and everyone around her got up and left class. Angelita dawdled. She'd decided it would be best to get to the cafeteria late and survey the scene. If it didn't look promising, she could always go to auto shop instead.

By the time she got to the cafeteria, the lines were long and the tables jammed with students. Kennin and Tito were not sitting at their usual hideout by the windows. Angelita scanned the tables and spotted the back of Mariel Lewis's head. Good. She was facing the other direction. That was a lucky break. Angelita continued to look around. When she didn't see Kennin or her brother, she looked at the lines. Kennin was standing in the burrito and nacho line. Angelita knew this was her opportunity. Mariel had her back turned, and her brother wasn't around.

She walked up to Kennin.

"Hi."

Kennin smiled when he saw her. "Hey."

Eager to start a conversation, Angelita almost blurted out that she'd waited for him at the bus stop that morning, then caught herself because she didn't want to come across as too eager. Instead, she said, "Sorry I couldn't drive you home last night."

"No problem," Kennin said. "I appreciated the offer."

The line inched forward. In her mind Angelita scrambled for things to talk about. She could have brought up the tsuiso that night, but she had a feeling he'd know that wasn't really why she'd come up to him in the line. So why not just get to the point?

"So . . . ," she began, "you think after you get your nachos you could meet me in the band room?"

It took Kennin a second to understand. Then he said, "Yeah, sure."

"Great," Angelita said. "See you in a minute."

Although Mariel Lewis may have had her back turned, that did not mean other girls at her table were not aware of what was going on, and they were more than eager to keep Mariel informed of Kennin's and Angelita's every move.

"She just left," one of them whispered as soon as Angelita left the cafeteria for the band room. Mariel twisted around and looked at Kennin standing alone on the burrito line. She herself had plans concerning Kennin that lunchtime. As soon as he came out of the burrito and nacho line, she planned to pay him a visit.

But several minutes later, when Kennin came out of the line with a cardboard tray of nachos, he didn't head for a table as Mariel had expected. Instead, he went out through the same door Angelita had left through earlier. Instantly Mariel knew she had to change her plans, but she couldn't act too quickly. Not when she had an image to maintain.

"He just got his lunch and left," one of the girls at the table reported.

Mariel shrugged as if she couldn't care less.

Angelita was sitting on a riser in the band room when Kennin came in. Other than the chairs, music stands, and large instruments like tubas, basses, and drums, the room was empty. Kennin sat down beside her and put his cardboard tray of nachos in his lap.

"Care for one?" he asked.

"No, thanks," Angelita said. Like most people, she lost her appetite when she got nervous.

Kennin ate a nacho. Angelita knew he was waiting.

"So, I want to ask you something," she said, her heart beating hard. "I never understood how we went from that night at your place to the way you've acted for the past two weeks. I mean, it seemed like everything changed so fast."

Kennin had had a feeling this was what she wanted to talk about. But he also knew that he couldn't tell her the truth—that Tito had warned him to stay away from her because he would only mess up her plans for the future. More than most people, Kennin understood how valuable the opportunity to get out was. How many times had he dreamed of having a chance like that himself? A chance to get out of that miserable trailer park. A chance to undo the stupidity that had led to Doug's death. A chance to have a normal family instead of a stripper sister and a convict father. Maybe he wasn't going to get that chance, but he'd be damned if he'd deny someone else the opportunity.

But if he couldn't tell her that, then what could he say?

The answer stepped through the band room door.

"Gee, sorry, didn't mean to interrupt," Mariel said, but instead of backing out of the doorway and leaving, she continued in. "Almost finished?" she asked Angelita.

Angelita stiffened. "What do you want?"

"Some time alone with him," Mariel replied. "Like you just had."

Angelita gave Kennin a look. The message was, *I can't tell her to get lost, but you can.*

Kennin hesitated. He knew what he was about to do would destroy any future he had with Angelita. Then again, according to Tito, he was going to destroy Angelita's future if he *didn't* do it.

"I'm sorry, Angelita," he said, though it killed him to say it. "But I think I'd better talk to Mariel."

Angelita couldn't believe it. Nor could she stop the tears that burst from her eyes as she jumped up and hurried out of the band room past a gloating, triumphant Mariel.

21

That night, before the tsuiso, Tito met Kennin on the corner near the Riveras' house. It was close to midnight when Kennin got there. Tito was standing under a streetlight with his arms crossed tightly and a frown on his face. He looked seriously pissed off. "What the hell happened with my sister?" he asked.

"I did what you wanted me to do, Tito," Kennin said.

"Yeah, but for *carajo*'s sake did you have to do it *that* way?"

"What way?" Kennin asked.

"Dissing her in front of Mariel Lewis and making her cry."

"That what she told you?" Kennin asked. Something small flapped overhead past the streetlight. It was the size of a bird, but it flew differently. *Probably a bat*, Kennin thought. He didn't like bats.

"Angelita didn't say nothing," Tito said. "That's just what I heard in the halls. But all I had to do was look at her to see that it was true."

"You said you didn't want me in her future," Kennin said. "I didn't have to agree, but I did. For her sake. So forgive me if it didn't go as smoothly as you might have liked."

"Okay, okay." Tito let his arms fall. He even patted Kennin on the shoulder. "You're right, dude. I guess I should appreciate what you did. So, you amped about tonight?"

Kennin raised a dubious eyebrow. Once again the bat flapped past overhead. He knew there was a logical reason for it. Bats ate the bugs that were attracted by the light. But he still didn't like it.

Tito assumed Kennin was bothered by something else. "Yeah, I know, you're a little freaked about the course. But guess what? So's everyone else. That levels the playing field. Don't worry, you're a better drifter than everyone else."

So he'd been told. Kennin looked around in the dark, wondering why they were standing on the corner.

"We're waiting for Raoul," Tito said.

Kennin frowned.

"You didn't think Angelita was gonna drive us after what happened today, did you?" Tito asked. "Come on, can you blame her if she doesn't want to see you right now? I just spent an hour begging her to let us use the 240 SX.

She wasn't gonna do it. I mean, why do you any favors, right?"

"Maybe because it's your life savings on the line, not mine," Kennin guessed.

"Well, duh, dude, but I still had to get on my frickin' knees and beg."

"So Raoul's giving us a ride up to the mountain," Kennin said. "But how do we get the car up there?"

"Angelita's driving it," Tito said. "She already left. She'll meet us up there."

It didn't make sense to Kennin. If Angelita didn't want to see him, why didn't she just let them take the car from here? Why bring it up to the mountain herself? And why get Cousin Raoul involved?

Again Tito seemed to know what he was thinking. "You're trying to figure it out? Okay, look, a few weeks ago you ran against Ian and won, right? So what happened next? They came up with some stupid reason why it shouldn't count. So now we gotta start all over again. And every time we start over again, there's another chance I'm gonna lose all my money. So that's why I asked Raoul to come tonight. It can't hurt to have some muscle around if those guys try to say this tsuiso don't count."

The bat flapped through the edges of the light again. Kennin looked up, wishing it would go away.

"What's wrong?" Tito asked. "What're you looking at?"

"Nothing," Kennin said.

A familiar-looking beat-up white van came around the corner and stopped. Inside, Tito's cousin Raoul waved at them. Raoul was a good-natured loser, currently out on parole after serving twenty-two months on a grand theft auto rap. He would have been back in prison already had it not been for Kennin, who a month before had saved his butt when Raoul, up to his old tricks, had boosted a brand-new Pontiac GTO that just happened to belong to the wife of the mayor.

Tito pulled open the van's door, and he and Kennin got in.

"Raoul, my man, wazup?" Tito said.

"Nothin, just hanging, workin', tryin' to keep my nose clean," Raoul replied.

Raoul had recently gotten into the gardening business. Or, as he called it, landscape architecture. The van smelled of dead grass and gasoline. In the back were a lawn mower, a leaf blower, some rakes, and a Weedwacker. In addition, there were four extra tires for the 240 SX, some folding chairs, the car jack, and the impact wrench. Kennin wasn't surprised to find a couple of empty beer cans rolling around as well.

"So, we goin' racing again?" Raoul asked.

"Damn right," said Tito. "Tonight Kennin's gonna blow everyone off the road and I'm gonna collect on all those bets." He patted Kennin on the shoulder. "Right, my man?"

"Right," Kennin replied, thinking back to Jack's warning

that he had to lose the second heat or face the consequences.

They headed out of town. Kennin sat silently in the back with the lawn mower and the spare tires and the empty beer cans rattling around. It bothered him that Derek knew about the heats tonight. It bothered him that Jack knew. Why had Derek told him not to run? Why did Jack want him to run, but tank the second heat?

Tito turned and looked over the front seat at him. "What's wrong?"

Kennin shrugged.

"It's just three heats, dude," Tito said. "Set 'em up, blow 'em off, and shut 'em down."

"Right." Kennin forced a smile on his face. Only it didn't feel right. And he wished he knew why.

22

"*What the hell* is this?" Chris Craven asked loudly. The scene at the top of the mountain was pure party. Under a crescent moon and a sky filled with glittering stars, dozens of cars lined both sides of the narrow road. Crowds of people were milling around, talking and laughing, sitting on their cars listening to music, drinking, and smoking. Kennin counted nearly seventy people and at least twenty-five cars. In the midst of them, Megs, Chris, Kennin, and the other drivers gathered.

"I guess the word got out," said Driftdog Dave.

"Might as well send the cops an open invitation," Chris muttered.

"Look, we're all here," said Megs. "We gonna drive or what?"

Chris glanced in Kennin's direction. It was interesting

that he never seemed to make a major decision without looking Kennin's way. Kennin nodded back.

"Yeah, we're gonna run," Chris announced. "Same lineup as last time. Kennin and Ian first."

Kennin and Tito walked back through the crowd toward the 240 SX. As promised, Angelita had brought the car up the mountain. Now she stood off to the side in the dark with her friend Marta and watched while Kennin started to jack up the rear end and Tito got the extra tires out of the van. Raoul sat nearby in a folding chair with a beer in his hand. He may have been available to give them a lift, but he wasn't about to work the pit crew.

From up and down the road came loud chatter, laughing, music, and the staccato rapport of electric impact wrenches. Kennin and Tito pulled the street tires off the 240 SX and put the drifting tires on, then dropped the car's rear end and started to tighten the lug nuts with the impact wrench. Meanwhile, Marta pulled a folding chair up beside Raoul. Angelita remained standing in the brush and rocks off by herself, silhouetted by the black, glittery night. Kennin gazed at her.

Tito paused from tightening the lug nuts. "She'll get over it."

Kennin didn't answer. Angelita wasn't the only one who had to get over it.

"You win tonight, you'll be doing her a big favor," Tito said.

"How's that?" Kennin asked.

"Dude, she's gonna sell this thing." Tito patted the 240 SX's bumper. "College, remember? She'll get more for a beater than a loser, right?"

Angelita glanced in their direction. It was difficult for Kennin to read her expression in the dark, but he had a feeling that drifting was the very last thing on her mind.

Cars were still coming up the mountain road. The first heat wouldn't go off until the word came from Mutt that the road was clear. One of the more recent arrivals was a familiar-looking bright red Lexus IS300. The car stopped next to Tito and Kennin. The window went down, and Mariel Lewis looked out at Kennin. "Hey, come here. I want to talk to you."

Kennin leaned in the open window. The sweet aroma of Mariel's perfume filled his nostrils. She was wearing a tight, low-cut top, and when she leaned across the passenger seat to talk to him, he got an eyeful. "Excited?" she asked.

"Depends on what you mean," Kennin said.

Up the road a car revved loudly. Kennin heard the _whoosh_ of the turbo and looked away.

"Hey, I was talking to you." Mariel had to get his attention again.

He looked back through the window again. "Yeah?"

"I hope you win tonight," she said.

"What about your boyfriend?" Kennin asked. "Don't you want him to win?"

Mariel's finely plucked eyebrows dipped with consternation. "How many times do I have to tell you, he's not my boyfriend."

"He seems to think you're his girlfriend," Kennin said.

"That's his problem," Mariel said. "How's *your* girlfriend?"

Kennin frowned. Mariel tilted her forehead, gesturing behind him. Kennin looked around and caught Angelita watching them. Tito's sister quickly looked away. Kennin turned back to Mariel. "I'm in the first heat and I gotta get ready. Catch you later."

"Anytime," Mariel replied.

"Okay, guys," Megs announced through the megaphone, "we're shutting down the road for the first heat. Ian and Kennin are up."

Kennin felt a tingling in his hands. His forehead felt warm. It was time to focus. He strapped himself into the 240 SX and pulled on his helmet. Tito and Raoul leaned in the car's window. "Ready to go?"

Kennin nodded and started the car. It roared to life and idled smoothly. Angelita had it tuned perfectly. He clutched and ran through the gears to familiarize himself with the sequences once again. Angelita had shortened the throw on the shift lever to make the shifting faster.

"Sounds good," Raoul said, the alcohol on his breath so strong it would have lit if you'd held a match to it.

"Should sound good," Tito said proudly. "Thing's about as perfect as a street-legal drift vehicle can be."

The nearby revving of an engine made Kennin jerk his head up. Ian in his white Cressida pulled up beside the 240 SX. He was wearing a blue racing helmet with orange and yellow flame stickers.

"Hey, how's the boat people's racing team?" he snickered.

"Ready to run your sorry butt off the road," Tito shot back.

"Big talk, little guy," Ian smirked, and turned his attention to Kennin. "Dry road tonight, pal. So no excuses."

"He wasn't the one who made the excuses last time," Tito pointed out. "You were."

Ian gritted his teeth. "Easy to talk tough when you got that wacko and his butterfly knife backing you up. We'll see how tough you are tomorrow in school."

Tito swallowed and grew quiet, as if realizing that Ian was right.

"First heat, let's go," Megs announced. "Cars to the starting line."

Ian revved the Cressida loudly and pulled away. The road was so narrow and crowded with onlookers that Kennin had to do a three-point U-turn to get the 240 SX aimed in the right direction. As he pulled up to the start line, out of the corner of his eye he caught Angelita's face in the crowd. People were shouting and hooting, but Angelita's expression was a mixture of concern and hope. There was no hint of anger. Kennin felt a dull ache. He would almost have preferred that she be angry at him. Seeing that she still cared only made it worse.

"Ready!" Megs shouted through the megaphone.

Both Ian and Kennin revved their engines. Only this time it wasn't for show.

"Get set!" Megs raised his hand in the air.

Screech! A split second before Megs brought his arm down, the sound of the Cressida's tires digging into the pavement caught Kennin by surprise. He popped his clutch, mostly for show, since Ian already had a lead of half a car length. The kid had jumped the gun, but Kennin had no intention of lodging a complaint. It was a desperate move on Ian's part. Maybe foolish, maybe not. Deep down Ian probably knew that if Kennin had gotten the lead early he would have left the white Cressida in his dust. By getting out in front, he had left himself open to Kennin pushing him hard from behind on the dangerous, narrow course.

Kennin pushed the 240 SX flat out, determined to tuck the Nissan as tight as possible into the turn beside the Cressida and bang out hard. The pressure would be on Ian. He was going to make the kid sweat.

Suddenly Ian went into an early e-drift, sliding the Cressida sideways. It caught Kennin by surprise and he twisted the wheel quickly, but he lost power correcting to avoid T-boning Ian's car.

Kennin muttered under his breath. For the second time, Ian had caught him off guard. This move had little to do with drifting and everything to do with trying to put Kennin on the defensive. It was a warning that Ian would drive unpredictably. Next time Kennin tried to push him, he'd have to worry not only about controlling the 240 SX, but about slamming into the Cressida as well. For the first time, Kennin actually found something about the guy to admire. What Ian lacked in driving skill he made up for with his willingness to risk everything to win.

Because he'd started his drift too early, Ian found himself slowing down and sideways in the middle of the turn. But that left no room for Kennin to get around him, and that was the whole point. In fact, Kennin almost swore he saw a grin on Ian's face as he fishtailed the Cressida around, then powered out of the turn and into the descending straightaway, weaving all over the road to warn Kennin that he would stop at nothing, including a crash, to prevent him from getting past.

It was the same thing with the next switchback. Ian wasn't exactly drifting. It was more of a power slide to get sideways in the corner, fishtailing wildly, making it impossible for Kennin to get past him without risking an accident.

It happened again through the next corner and the next, Ian power-sliding the Cressida all over the road, getting in the way and blocking any chance for Kennin to get past. They headed into another long, narrow straightaway. Ian showed some hesitation here, as if he was worried about going into the next corner too fast. Kennin could have passed him, but Ian hogged the middle of the road, not giving him room on either side to get by.

Frustration began to simmer in Kennin's veins, but he forced himself to stay cool. Getting him angry was no doubt part of Ian's plan. He was waiting for Kennin to get aggravated, hoping he'd try a move where there wasn't enough room. Then all it would take was a little nudge from the Cressida to push the 240 SX off the edge or into a boulder.

Kennin plowed through a hard right, bracing himself against the door with his left leg. Ahead of him, Ian slowed even more into the next set of turns. Either he was unsure of the course layout, or he was purposely taunting Kennin. The Cressida didn't even have enough speed to drift through the second corner in this set, but since they were now midway through the heat, and halfway down the course, Ian must have known there'd be no one watching in the dark. But slowing down that much had its disadvantages as well, and Kennin was beginning to formulate a strategy.

When they came out of that set of turns and into a short straightaway before the next set, Ian once again placed the Cressida dead center in the road. Kennin weaved the 240 SX from side to side as if he were desperately trying to find a way to get around the lead car. As they entered the turns, Ian again got sideways, slowing down and blocking Kennin's way. Kennin feinted as if to go inside, and when Ian began to counter by fishtailing the Cressida, Kennin e-braked hard, then dropped the hammer and went high around the outside. The next thing Ian knew, he and Kennin were side by side coming out of the turn.

Ahead were the S-turns through the narrow ravine lined by those tall walls of rock.

23

Turbos whining side by side, the white Cressida and blue 240 SX shot toward the ravine.

The road ahead was narrowing.

Kennin looked to his left and saw Ian swivel his head and stare back. It was a game of chicken now.

The rocky, jagged walls of the ravine rose up on either side as the two cars flew past the sign warning them to yield to uphill traffic.

Ian and Kennin glanced at each other again. Gloved hands in white-knuckle grips on the wheels. Neither of them letting up for an instant.

The road continued to narrow. Ahead the rocky walls of the ravine, illuminated in the headlights, pressed inward. Kennin redlined the 240 SX. Adrenaline pulsed through his veins. Everything was in ultraclear focus. The cracks in the asphalt roadbed. The deep scrapes in the rocky walls where other cars had misjudged.

As the road continued to narrow, the space between the cars narrowed as well. Out of the corner of his eye, Kennin saw Ian turn and look at him again. Derek and Jack both said Kennin had a good poker face. Now was the time to show it to Ian.

Clank! The cars missed and bounced away from each other. Without taking his foot off the gas, Kennin fought the wheel for control. In the Cressida Ian did the same. The dark rocky walls ahead appeared to rise and narrow.

Ian glanced at Kennin again.

Kennin leaned forward in his seat, as if willing the 240 SX ahead. This time he intentionally didn't look back at Ian. He was going into that ravine flat out no matter what.

There was a sudden loud screaming *screech*, and the Cressida disappeared behind him in a cloud of white tire smoke. A split second later Kennin drifted into the first S-turn and then the next before gunning out of the ravine and down the final straightaway, finally crossing the finish line, where Mutt gave him a wave.

The heat was over. Kennin had won.

He pulled the 240 SX off to the side of the road, killed the engine and lights, and sat in the dark, letting his body go limp. For the first time he became aware of sweat dripping down his forehead, and the cramped sensation in his hands from gripping the wheel so tight. His heart was banging. He

pulled off his helmet and let his head go back against the seat. It had been a full-on run. Ian may have been a crappy drifter, but he'd put up a hell of a fight.

Rap! Rap! The sound of someone banging on his window snapped Kennin out of his reverie. Ian was standing outside, still wearing his helmet, glowering and gesturing at him to get out of the car.

"Get out, Chinaboy! I mean now, you chicken-ass Jap!"

Kennin put both hands on the inside of the door and pushed it open as hard as he could . . . right into Ian. It knocked the guy backward. Ian lost his footing and fell on his butt on the road, but quickly jumped to his feet and charged, head down like a bull. And just like a bullfighter, Kennin stepped to the side, grabbed the guy's shoulders, and slammed him helmet first into the side of the Nissan.

Thwunk! Ian's head hit the side of the car so hard it made Kennin wince. He was sure he'd put a dent in the door. Ian collapsed facedown on the road. Even wearing the racing helmet, the impact had stunned him.

In the distance Kennin heard the redline whine and screeching as the next two cars went off. Up the mountain he could see the headlights slanting down the straightaways and then skidding around the switchbacks.

Still prone on the ground, Ian groaned. Mutt came through the dark. "What happened to him?"

"Don't know," Kennin said. "He must have tripped and fallen or something."

The whining engines and screeching tires were getting louder. The sounds echoed as the cars skidded through the S-turns in the ravine, the headlights brightening the rocky walls. A second later two sets of headlights burst out of the dark, one close behind the other. The cars raced to the finish line, bumper to bumper, Chris's *Slide or Die* narrowly beating out Driftdog Dave.

The cars pulled off to the sides of the road. Just as Kennin had done, both drivers killed their engines and sat in their cars for a moment before getting out. Finally Chris and Driftdog got out of their cars, pulled off their helmets, and walked toward each other. Unlike Ian's reaction to losing, Driftdog took off his racing gloves and shook Chris's hand.

"Good heat, dude," Driftdog said.

"You almost got me on the third corner," Chris said.

"Couldn't hold that line," Driftdog said, shaking his head regretfully.

Meanwhile, Ian got to his hands and knees. "Oh, man," he groaned, sitting on the road surface. He pulled off his helmet and held his head in his hands. By now Chris and Driftdog noticed Kennin and Ian and crossed the road toward them. Mutt was on the cell phone telling Megs the course was clear for the next heat.

"What happened?" Chris asked.

Kennin pointed down at Ian. "To him or in the heat?"

"Both," Driftdog Dave said.

Before Kennin could answer, Ian muttered, "Dickhead cheated."

In the dark Chris frowned. "How?"

Ian slowly got to his feet and glared at Kennin. "You crazy mother. You coulda killed us both!"

Now Mutt joined them. "What's the problem?"

"The jerk cheated," Ian said. "I was ahead almost the whole way. You can't count that finish."

Chris looked back and forth between Kennin and Ian. "Why not?"

"We got to that spot in the ravine where it narrows," Ian said, pointing at Kennin, "and this dillweed wouldn't back off."

"I thought you said you were ahead," Chris said.

"I—I was," Ian stammered. "Up till then."

"I don't get it," Mutt said.

"We went in side by side," Kennin said.

"I was ahead," Ian insisted. "This dipstick should have backed off."

"If you were ahead," Chris said, "it wouldn't have mattered."

Driftdog and Mutt exchanged doubtful looks. Ian's story made no sense. Chris bowed his head and stared at the road. Kennin imagined he was stuck between a rock and a hard place. He wanted his friend to win, but it really didn't matter who was or wasn't ahead when they entered the ravine. The only thing that mattered was who crossed the finish line first.

Chris looked at Ian and shook his head. "Sorry, man, there's nothing I can do." He turned away and walked back to his car.

Ian turned to Kennin. "Way to go, cheater."

Kennin turned away and started back toward the Nissan.

"Hey," Ian said behind him.

Kennin stopped.

"Watch your back," the red-haired kid warned.

24

Kennin waited with the other drivers at the bottom of the mountain while the last two battles were run. The drivers stood in the dark beside their cars listening to the tires squeal and watching the headlights swing. With the moon just a crescent, it was even darker than usual. The first round of heats ended. They'd started with eight drivers. Now there were four. After the next round of heats there would be two.

Mutt got off his cell phone. "Okay, guys, it's clear. Go back up."

Kennin and the other three winners from the first heats got into their cars and headed up. While some of the losers had headed back toward Las Vegas, he noticed that Ian got into the white Cressida to drive back up with the rest of them.

When Kennin got to the top of the mountain, the scene was even more crowded than before. There were people everywhere, drinking, playing music, smoking. It was pretty obvious that the actual tsuiso was the last thing on most of their minds. Kennin had to drive up and down the crowded mountain road twice before he spotted Tito in the crowd.

"So how'd it go?" Tito asked glumly.

"I'm back up here, aren't I?"

Tito didn't answer. It seemed a little odd to Kennin. The guy should have been amped that there were only two more races to go before he'd collect all the winnings on those bets.

"See any place where I can park?" Kennin asked.

Tito was gazing off into the dark and didn't seem to hear him.

"Hey," Kennin said to get his attention. "I want to park."

"Don't bother," Tito said. "You'll be running again in a minute."

Angelita came up behind her brother and looked over his shoulder at Kennin. Her face was expressionless. Kennin assumed she was curious to know how the heat went and how the car handled.

"It looked like Ian got out ahead of you in the beginning," she said. "Where'd you pass him?"

"At the ravine," Kennin said.

Angelita stared at him and her brow furrowed. She glanced at the Nissan, as if to make sure she hadn't missed any body damage. Kennin was glad it was dark. He'd wait until later to explain the dings on the driver's side where the

240 SX had tapped the Cressida, and the dent where Ian's head had slammed into the side of the door.

"How'd you pass Ian at the ravine?" she asked.

"We were tied going in," Kennin said.

It only took a moment for the implication to sink in. "You played chicken with my car?" The disapproval in Angelita's voice was audible.

"Sometimes that's what a tsuiso is about," Kennin said.

"I don't know," Angelita said. "It's one thing if this car gets dinged by accident. But I didn't build it just so you could go out and take crazy chances."

"I know that," Kennin said.

"You sure?" Angelita said.

"I knew Ian would bag it," Kennin said.

"How?" Angelita asked.

Kennin paused, then said, "Because he was driving his own car, and he knew I wasn't."

Angelita scowled for a moment. "You mean, since he was driving his own car you knew he'd bail because he couldn't risk smashing it up? But because you were driving someone else's car he assumed you didn't care?"

"I cared," Kennin explained. "I just knew I had a psychological advantage."

"Dude, that is harsh," Tito said.

Angelita rolled her eyes unhappily at Kennin. "As far as I'm concerned, you got lucky. You don't try that again, understand? Not with my car."

Kennin nodded. A loud laugh rose up nearby from a bunch of guys standing around with beers in their hands.

"Is this crazy?" Tito said. "I don't think half these people even know there's a tsuiso going down with big money on the line. They probably think this is just some mountaintop party."

"A big party that's gonna bring the cops," Angelita said sourly.

Tito didn't answer. His expression had changed, and he was staring at something in the dark. Kennin followed the direction of his gaze. In the crowd a dozen yards away, Derek Jamison, Mike Mercado's right-hand man, was talking to Chris. Chris was listening and nodding.

"What's he doing here?" Kennin asked.

Tito shook his head slowly. "There's crap going down here like you wouldn't believe."

Through the windshield of the 240 SX, Kennin watched as Derek and Chris both turned and looked at him. Then they turned away and continued talking. Kennin assumed Derek was up there checking out drivers for the Babylon drift team. But now something else had caught his eye: the silhouette in the dark of someone wearing a black cowboy hat.

25

Jack the jackass came out of the shadows and stopped beside the car. "Clear out for a moment, kids," he said to Tito and Angelita, who backed away.

"Who's that?" Angelita whispered to her brother.

Tito shrugged and didn't answer. Angelita told herself she shouldn't care. Not after what had happened earlier that day in the band room with Mariel. As far as she was concerned, Kennin could go to hell. The only reason she had come tonight was to make sure her car ran well. The only reason she wanted Kennin to win was so that her idiot brother could collect on his bets. After tonight she was through with all of this. She'd sell the car and focus on finishing the school year and going off to college.

Meanwhile, Jack the jackass leaned into the window of the 240 SX and spoke in a soft growl. "Congratulations on your win, boy."

Kennin didn't answer. In the dark, Jack couldn't see Kennin's hands tighten around the steering wheel.

"You ain't forgot what happens next, have you?" Jack asked.

Kennin shook his head.

"Good for you, boy." Jack reached in and patted him on the helmet. "Now you be a good little brother and do just what I told you. Your sister'll be mighty appreciative."

Jack strolled away into the dark.

Angelita watched the whole thing. She knew something wasn't right. She could feel it. There were all these grown men who'd never been around for a tsuiso before. They had serious expressions and looked like more than casual bystanders. She told herself she shouldn't care, but she did. She looked at her brother. "Who was that?"

"Forget about it," Tito answered.

"Is something going on here?" she asked.

"I said forget about it," said Tito. "Besides, what do you care after what happened this afternoon?"

Her brother was right, Angelita thought. She really had to stop caring.

"Okay, listen up," Megs announced through the megaphone. "It's time for the semifinal heats. First heat'll be Chris against Micky Shift 'n' Slide."

"That means Kennin will be up against Carlos," Tito said.

Carlos drove *Die Screaming*, a yellow Honda 2000. He

pretty much stuck to himself and didn't talk much to the other drivers. But everyone said he was a good drifter.

It took a while to clear the partiers away from the start area so that Chris and Micky could line up. Chris was in his bright red *Slide or Die*. Micky drove a black supercharged Chevy Camino. Kennin got out of the 240 SX to stretch his legs. He pulled off his helmet and leaned against the car in the dark, breathing in the cool mountain air.

On the cell phone Megs got the okay from Mutt to start the heat.

Megs brought the megaphone to his lips and raised his arm. "Ready! Set!"

He brought his arm down.

The scream of spinning tires filled the air along with twin clouds of white smoke as the cars leaped off the starting line. A moment later two sets of red taillights disappeared around the first turn. All that remained was the high-pitched whine of the engines and the shrieking of tires.

As the sounds of the cars faded and were replaced once again by the noise of the partiers, Tito came over and leaned against the car beside Kennin. Together they gazed at the crowd. Raoul was slumped in his folding chair, surrounded by empty beer cans and looking wasted. Not far from him, Angelita and Marta were talking to a couple of guys Kennin had never seen before. He assumed they were from a different school.

"Crazy scene, huh?" Tito said.

"Yeah."

"You know, maybe this organized drifting thing with Mercado could work," Tito said. "I mean, look at the crowd."

"Half of them don't even know there's a tsuiso going on," Kennin said.

"Maybe it doesn't matter," Tito said. "As long as half the crowd does know, the other half'll follow. I mean, if this was a sanctioned event, I bet the gate would be pretty impressive."

"The gate?" Kennin repeated.

"Yeah, you know, the money they'd make from the ticket sales," Tito said. "They call that the gate. And that doesn't include the merchandising and refreshments. And then there's ad revenue and maybe even cable coverage. There could be some real money in this."

Kennin gave him an amused look. "I didn't know you were such a businessman."

"Hey, there's a lot you don't know about me," Tito said.

Kennin frowned. "What are you talking about?"

"I'm just saying, nobody ever bothers to take me seriously, but maybe it's time they did," Tito said. "Right now I see an opportunity that's a lot bigger than this stupid tsuiso. You don't want to miss it and then wind up kicking yourself later, right?"

Kennin thought of his sister. At that moment back in Las Vegas, Shinchou was probably dancing at Rustler's and hating every second of it because she'd once thought there was "an opportunity" too. Maybe opportunities weren't as simple or obvious as they appeared. And since when was running tsuisos an "opportunity"? It was supposed to be about good driving and good cars. All the rest—drift teams, gates, ticket sales, crowds—was a lot of BS.

Through the crowd Kennin saw Megs flip open his phone. He was probably calling Mutt to get the results of Chris's heat. A few moments later he snapped the phone closed and lifted the megaphone to his lips. "Okay, Kennin and Carlos, you're up."

"Hey, Megs, who won?" Tito called.

"Who do you think?" Megs called back.

"Guess that means Chris," Tito said while Kennin strapped his helmet on and got into Angelita's 240 SX. He was pulling on the harness when the sweet scent of perfume drifted into his nostrils.

Mariel leaned into his window. "Well, how do you like that?" she cooed seductively. "You win against *Die Screaming* and it'll be the showdown everyone's been waiting for."

"I'll keep that in mind," Kennin said.

Mariel lightly traced a finger across the bare skin above her low-cut top. "Keep this in mind, too, *papi*."

Standing a dozen feet away and watching the whole thing, Angelita felt her blood start to boil. She couldn't stand the way that slut Mariel strutted her stuff. Forgetting that she'd resolved to have nothing more to do with Kennin, she quickly went over and stuck her head in the passenger-side window of the Nissan.

"I meant what I said before," she said.

Kennin quickly turned his head, surprised to see her.

"I want this car back in one piece," Angelita said.

"I hear you," Kennin answered.

Angelita stepped back from the window. Kennin put the 240 SX in gear and pulled away, leaving an empty space between Angelita and Mariel. The two girls glared at each other.

"Didn't you get the message this afternoon?" Mariel asked. "He's not interested."

Angelita felt her eyes narrow with anger and her hands ball into fists. That damned *puta* was so full of herself that it made Angelita furious. Rarely had she felt this much hate for anyone. Even though Angelita knew it was probably best if she and Kennin stayed apart, she wanted to do whatever it took to keep Mariel away from him too.

Kennin pulled up to the start line. Carlos drove the yellow Honda 2000 up beside him. Kennin nodded at the other driver.

Megs raised his arm. "Ready! Set!"

Both cars revved loudly.

The arm came down.

Kennin popped the clutch and felt the g-forces push him back against the racing bucket. Both cars took off. *Die Screaming* was even with him.

Even as Kennin began his first feint, he knew he would let Carlos win. When you thought about it, the decision was simple. Tito may have been a friend, but Shinchou was family. Tito would lose his bets, but Kennin had never wanted him to make those bets in the first place. Tito had gone ahead and made them without asking him. And what Tito would lose in money, Shinchou would gain in time and less stress. A pretty easy choice, when you thought about it.

But while he didn't have to win this heat, his pride made him want to keep it close. He and *Die Screaming* went into the first corner side by side. Coming out, Kennin got half a length ahead, but the lead was negligible because the next turn was a right and *Die Screaming* had the inside. They went through that drift and now *Die Screaming* had the half-car-length lead. Both cars redlined toward the next switchback, again entering it even.

Only this time Kennin had the inside and came out ahead of the Honda. Against every instinct, Kennin eased off and kept the battle close. Carlos wasn't a bad drifter, but Kennin knew that he could have lost him if he'd felt like it. As they went through the next switchback, Kennin felt his frustration growing. He let opportunity after opportunity pass while reminding himself that for Shinchou's sake he had to lose.

They went through another curve, and Kennin lost another opportunity to leave Carlos inhaling his exhaust. They had one corner left and then the S-turns through the narrow ravine. Kennin eased up on the accelerator. All Carlos had to do was keep a tight line around the corner and the tsuiso was his.

But Carlos went into the turn too tight, as if certain this was where Kennin would try to snake him. He started to oversteer, and only a radical correction saved him from ending in a donut. But the correction also sent *Die Screaming* far off the apex of the curve.

Suddenly there was a huge opening right before Kennin's eyes. In that instant, pure instinct took hold. Kennin couldn't help it. It was in his nature to fight and win. And besides, thanks to Carlos's mistake, there was no way he could *not* take the opportunity without it looking like he was intentionally tanking.

The next thing Kennin knew, he was in front going into the ravine. *Die Screaming* was three car lengths behind him, with no way to catch up or pass. Nor was there any way Kennin could now give up the lead in the final straightaway without it looking incredibly obvious.

Seconds later he burst out of the ravine and down the straightaway past Mutt. The battle was over. He'd won.

Jack the jackass would not be happy.

26

At the bottom he and Carlos shook hands. Carlos got back into the Honda and headed home. Across the road in the dark, Chris was leaning against *Slide or Die* with his arms crossed. Kennin turned and faced him. The two drivers were alone in the dark.

"Just as everyone predicted," Chris said. "You and me in the finals. And in nearly identical cars with pretty close to identical mods. I guess if there was gonna be a battle that would be a pure test of a driver's skills, this'll be it."

Mutt stepped between them. "Okay, guys, it's clear to go back up."

Chris gave Kennin a nod. "See you up top."

Kennin drove the 240 SX back up the mountain in the dark. He understood that what he'd just done went against everything he thought was right. He'd been trying to tell himself that winning wasn't that important. That pride was a weakness, not a strength. But that opening presented itself, and his true nature surged up from inside him. He wanted to win, and he was willing to risk whatever he had to do it.

But now he really had to lose the next heat, for Shinchou's sake.

At the top of the mountain the partying continued. People spilled into the road, blocking the way. Loud music and laughter filled the air. In the Nissan, Kennin waited patiently, slowly nudging the car forward through the crowd. He found himself searching the faces for Angelita's. It was dark and he didn't see her. Megs came out of the milling bodies. "Nice win, Kennin," he said. "Listen, I need to talk to you and Chris."

Now that the car had stopped moving, it was surrounded by people. "Where should I park?" Kennin asked.

"Don't bother," Megs said. "Just turn around and leave it. I'll help you."

With Megs waving people out of the way, Kennin managed to turn the car around on the narrow road. He pulled beside *Slide or Die*, then got out and started to squeeze through the milling crowd. Most people moved out of the way as Kennin pressed past them. But one body didn't. Kennin looked up and saw the cowboy hat.

"Thought we had an agreement," Jack snarled.

Kennin had nothing to say, and started to go around him, but now an even larger body blocked his path. Kennin recognized the silver medallion. It was the big, bald goon, Tiny.

Jack moved close to Kennin and growled into his ear. "You pay attention when I'm talking to you, boy. Now, we had a deal. I don't like it when people don't hold up their half of the bargain."

Kennin remained silent. The sound of laughter and music and a ratcheting impact wrench was in his ears.

"I need to hear that you're gonna lose this next race, understand?" Jack practically had to shout. His hot breath stank of cigarettes. "I got a hell of a lot more than your measly winnings riding on this, boy. And not only that, but your sister's gonna be one unhappy little chippy if you don't start cooperating pronto. Now I want to hear it straight from the horse's mouth. You're gonna lose this next race, right?"

Kennin remained tight-lipped. He'd decide for himself what he wanted to do, and the more Jack pushed, the less likely he was to go along.

"Say it, boy," Jack snarled.

"Hey, what is this?" Megs, Chris, and a couple of the other guys came through the crowd, giving Jack and Tiny curious looks.

It was Jack's turn to be tight-lipped. Obviously, he wasn't about to explain that he was trying to fix the tsuiso. Instead, he gave Kennin one last warning look, and then he and Tiny backed away into the dark crowd.

Not far away, Angelita had watched the whole thing. The guy in the cowboy hat had clearly been angry. But

Kennin had won. Then . . . was cowboy-hat guy angry about that? Why? And what had he just said to Kennin?

Meanwhile, Megs was trying to talk to Kennin and Chris.

"Listen, we gotta get this last heat off fast," Megs said, half yelling. "Half these people don't even know there's a tsuiso going on, and the other half are so blitzed they don't care. I'm freaked about getting you guys up to the line and then having some bozo cross your path just as you're taking off. So I'm telling you up front it's gonna have to be a real quick start. Be ready for it, okay?"

Chris and Kennin nodded.

"But no jumping off the line, right?" Megs went on.

"Right."

"Okay, guys, let's do it."

Kennin walked back through the crowd toward the cars. The bodies were packed so tightly together that he couldn't even see the two Nissans. Music was booming and the sound of an impact wrench reverberated through the air. Suddenly Kennin had a feeling something wasn't right.

Someone blocked his path. It was Ian, swaying slightly and clutching a can of Red Bull, no doubt fortified with vodka. He was wearing his baseball cap backward, trying his best to look like a gangsta.

"So this is it, tofu boy," Ian growled, slurring his words. "The main event. The one everyone's been waiting for."

Kennin was still trying to figure out what was bothering him, but Ian was distracting.

"You shouldn't even be in this tsuiso," Ian said ominously, as if he was looking to pick another fight.

"Not now," Kennin said. "I've got a heat to run."

He tried to go around him, but Ian spread his arms. "Frickin' cheater," he grumbled.

Megs saw what was happening and came over.

"You can talk about it later, okay?" Megs said. "Right now Kennin's got to get ready."

"I want a rematch," Ian insisted.

"So what else is new?" Megs asked impatiently.

While Megs tried to pacify Ian, Kennin watched the drunken football player's hands. Megs was a scrawny guy and would be no match if Ian wanted to fight. When Ian's right hand suddenly balled into a fist, Kennin grabbed Megs's arm and yanked.

Megs stumbled out of reach just as Ian threw a punch. Pulled by the momentum, Ian staggered forward, then caught his balance and wheeled around to deliver his next punch to Kennin's jaw. But Kennin ducked under it and hit Ian hard in the ribs.

"Oof!" Ian grunted, and doubled over. A circle instantly formed around Kennin and Ian. People began to shout, "Fight!" and the crowd quickly grew larger. Just as he had the last time they'd faced each other, Ian lowered his head and charged like a bull. Kennin jumped to the side, but tripped over something. The next thing he knew, he was falling. Someone had tripped him, either purposely or accidentally.

Kennin hit the rough pavement shoulder first. He rolled over and saw Ian's boots coming toward him. The kid meant to kick him in the face. Kennin just managed to roll away as the boot passed his face so close he could feel the breeze it created.

He jumped to his feet. The crowd had formed a tight circle and was chanting, "Fight! Fight!" The shouting, the music, and the impact wrench were deafening. Ian and Kennin circled each other. Kennin felt like the blood in his veins had been replaced with pure adrenaline. His heart was beating like a piston. This fight was for blood. If Ian had connected with that kick, Kennin could have been killed.

"Come on, gook, let's see what ya got," Ian taunted him, waving his fists.

Kennin kept circling, looking for an opportunity. Out of the corner of his eyes he saw faces in the crowd. Mariel with wide, excited eyes. Jack watching impassively, as if it was just another fight and no big deal. Tiny looked on eagerly. Megs tried to squeeze through the crowd to break the fight up, but Chris grabbed him and held him back.

"Come on, Jap boy," Ian taunted. "Too bad your friend with the butterfly knife is passed out drunk. Guess you'll have to take care of yourself this time. Bring it on."

"For once in your life, why don't you just shut up and fight?" Kennin shot back.

Ian's eyes widened and he charged, as if he only knew

one way to fight, and that was to put his head down and barrel into his opponent. The last two times Kennin had been relatively gentle, but after Ian tried to kick him in the head, he wasn't feeling quite so kindly. This time Kennin caught him by the shoulders and brought his knee up under the guy's chin. He heard a *crunch!* as his knee made contact with Ian's jaw. Ian grunted and fell down face-first on the road.

The crowd went silent. Ian lay motionless on the asphalt.

Kennin felt a sudden, nauseated sensation. What if he'd really hurt the guy? Or even killed him?

27

On the ground Ian stirred. He slowly lifted his head, then sat up, holding his chin in both hands. Kennin felt a wave of relief. Now that the fight was over, the crowd started to break up. A couple of guys bent over Ian to see if he was okay. The red-haired guy just sat there with his face in his hands, dazed.

"Way to go, dude." Driftdog Dave patted Kennin on the back.

"That loser deserved it," added someone else.

Kennin turned toward the 240 SX. A dozen feet away Jack the jackass stared at him coldly. People backed out of the way and made room for Kennin. It seemed quieter now. The music wasn't as loud. The ratcheting of the impact wrench was gone. Kennin still felt uneasy, as if there was something he should have known . . . something he was missing.

Fingers lightly touching his shoulder distracted him. He stopped and found Mariel. She leaned toward him and pressed her lips against his ear. Kennin felt a tingle run down his spine and goose bumps on his arms as her warm breath enveloped his ear. "Hope you win, _papi_," she whispered. "I'll be waiting for you."

"Come on, Kennin," Megs called. "Chris is ready to go."

Kennin reached the starting line where the two 240 SXs were lined up. Chris, wearing a red Bell helmet, was already in the gleaming red _Slide or Die_. Kennin got into Angelita's dull blue version of the same car. They exchanged a last look and nod. Someone leaned in the window while Kennin buckled in. Kennin expected it to be Tito, but it was Driftdog.

"This is it, dude," Driftdog said in a low voice. "The big enchilada. I hope you smoke that guy bad."

"Thanks," Kennin said.

Driftdog reached in and patted Kennin on the helmet, then backed away from the window. Kennin tugged his driving gloves on tight. When he looked back up, Angelita had taken Driftdog's place in the open window.

Kennin was surprised, and unexpectedly glad to see her. "Hey," he said, and felt a smile curl onto his lips.

"Listen," she said. "I know I sounded harsh before—"

"It's okay," Kennin cut her short. "I understand. You had good reason."

Angelita frowned. "I don't get it. Today in the band room . . ."

"Things aren't always what they seem," Kennin said.

"Kennin!" Megs yelled. "Come on, dude. You ready?"

Angelita reached in and put her hand on Kennin's arm. "I really do hope you win. Just be careful, okay?"

Kennin nodded. "Thanks. I really appreciate that."

Despite herself, Angelita leaned farther into the window. It was just going to be a kiss on the cheek. That was all. Just to wish him good luck.

But when she came close, Kennin reached up and gently turned her face toward him.

They kissed.

"Hey, hey! I thought we had an understanding!" Seemingly out of nowhere, Tito stuck his head into the passenger window and interrupted them.

Angelita frowned and stared at Kennin. Their faces were inches away. "What understanding? What's he talking about?"

"Later," Kennin said.

Angelita backed away. Kennin pulled down the visor on his helmet.

"Drivers ready?" Megs said through the megaphone.

Kennin started the 240 SX and revved the engine. The needle on the tach jumped. Once again the crowd noise grew louder. Maybe it was Kennin's imagination, but he thought he could feel the excitement in the air, as if the crowd actually was aware that this was the final heat of the tsuiso.

Megs stepped between the two cars, holding the mega-phone to his lips, his other arm raised high over his head.

One hand on the steering wheel, the other on the shift, Kennin reminded himself to be ready for a quick start.

"Ready! Set!"

Kennin and Chris revved their engines, drowning out every other sound.

Megs brought his hand down and Kennin and Chris took off, tires squealing and smoking.

The second the 240 SX broke traction, Kennin sensed something was wrong. There was a shimmy in the steering. He couldn't be certain, but it felt like the right front wheel. It was hard to focus because the g-forces were pressing him back, and he and Chris were dead even. It could have been something minor, but it also could have meant trouble.

The cars gained speed and the shimmy grew worse. The whole front end was vibrating. They were coming into the first corner. Kennin had to make a decision. Did he take a chance that whatever was wrong wouldn't affect the car enough to matter? Or did he bag the run now? But what if he quit and there was nothing really wrong? What kind of fool would he look like then? How much abuse would he have to take from Ian and Chris and the rest of them? What happened to the guy who said he didn't care what people thought?

They went into the first curve, a right. Both drivers countersteered, then broke traction and swung right. Kennin felt a tremendous vibration rattle the length of the car.

Then something let go. The right front dropped and the car slid sideways, then began to spin. Kennin thought he saw a wheel bounce away into the darkness. The car was spinning, the remaining three wheels shrieking. Yellow and orange sparks flew where the right front dragged on the pavement. Everything felt like slow motion. Kennin was getting jerked hard to the left, then the right. Sitting in the car was like being on a carnival ride. Going around and around. Kennin braced himself against the g-forces pulling at him. Still spinning, the car left the road and started to buck and bounce over the gravel. Pebbles, rocks, brush, and dust flew in the air, and the roar sounded like a landslide. Strapped into the seat and fighting the wheel, Kennin had a 360-degree view as the headlights illuminated rocks, gravel, and brush whipping past.

The impact wrench, he suddenly realized. *That was what had been bothering him. There'd been no reason for it.*

In the headlights the brush was taller, the rocks bigger . . .

The car spun past one boulder.

Then . . . *Crash!*

Todd Strasser is the author of more than one hundred twenty books for teens and middle graders, including the bestselling Help! I'm Trapped In . . . series, and numerous award-winning YA novels, including *The Wave*, *Give a Boy a Gun*, and *Can't Get There from Here*. As a boy, Todd was a fan of international Formula One grand prix and GT racers such as Graham Hill, Jim Clark, and Jackie Stewart. An avid go-cart driver in his youth, Todd went on to drive a variety of motorcycles and sports cars before marriage and children slowed him down.

Learn more about Todd at www.toddstrasser.com.

sidewayz glory

Don't miss the thrilling conclusion of
Todd Strasser's DriftX trilogy.

"Looks like you found me," Kennin said.

Derek pushed open the Hummer's door and stepped down. Without a word Tony came out of the valet office and parked the car.

"Let's take a walk," Derek said.

"What about me?" Tito asked.

"You stay," Derek said. It was obvious he was in a bad mood. He and Kennin left the garage and started to stroll down the sidewalk past the tourists and out-of-town gamblers who would soon be going home broke.

"Not living in the trailer park anymore?" Derek asked.

"What can I do for you, Mr. Jamison?" Kennin cut to the chase.

"It's time to stop screwing around, kid," Derek said. "Mr. Mercado made you a very nice offer, and it's time you accepted it."

"I told Mr. Mercado I'd think about it," Kennin replied.

"Let explain something to you, kid," Derek said. "People don't tell Mr. Mercado they'll think about things, okay? You do what he says or you suffer the consequences. Now he wants a rivalry between you and Chris Craven, okay? Nobody wants to watch the Yankees play the Colorado Rockies, but when the Yankees play the Red Sox, you can't find a seat. Michigan versus Ohio State, Auburn versus Alabama, USC versus UCLA. That's what brings people out. Now, I've known Mike Mercado a long time, and I've never seen him be this generous before. That's not a five-grand *loan* he's talking about. It's a frickin' gift. No one thumbs his nose at a gift from Mike Mercado."

"I guess he could break my other leg," Kennin said. "Or is it time for that shallow grave in the desert?"

Derek let out a big sigh. "All right, kid, let me explain it to you in a different way. Car washers are a dime a dozen. Mr. Mercado don't need you to wash cars. He can find a hundred other kids to do that. And he definitely don't need kids who borrow his clients' BMWs for a few hours without permission. So there's your choice, kid, either Mr. Mercado thinks of you as a drifter on his team, or as a car washer who tends to borrow cars that ain't his."

Kennin didn't like to be threatened. He didn't see the point.

"You know, Mr. Jamison," he said, "you're right that car washers are a dime a dozen, but the flip side of that is that there are a hundred other jobs around here that pay just as badly. So if I lose this one, chances are pretty good I'll find another one."

Like an experienced boxer, Derek came right back with another punch. "You know, kid, you're tough, and I admire that in you, but you haven't learned to recognize when the cards are stacked against you, okay? And this is one of those times. So which card would you like me to play next? How about the 'I know where your sister is' card? And here's another one. I know there's a slimeball pimp and drug dealer who's looking real hard for her. How's that hand sound?"

Kennin stopped walking and gave Derek an astonished look.

"Come on, kid, you're smarter than that," Derek said. "You must've figured out by now that you can't keep a secret in this town."

"Tito told you?" Kennin asked.

Derek shook his head.

"Then how?"

Derek gave him a steady look and said nothing.

"If you know, maybe a lot of people know," Kennin said. "Maybe it's not a secret anymore. So my doing anything for you won't help anyway."

Derek gave Kennin a weary look. "I guess there's one way to find out. You willing to give it a try?"

Kennin didn't have to think about it for long. "If I take Mr. Mercado's five thousand and build a drift car, can you swear that no one else will find out where my sister is?"

"I can swear that they won't find out from me," Derek said.

Kennin knew he'd been backed into a corner. "Okay," he said. "But so help me, if anything happens to my sister, I am coming after you."

Derek grinned. "I admire your spunk, kid." He reached into his jacket pocket and pulled out an envelope. "This is for the car and nothing else, understand? I find out a penny of this money went anywhere else, the deal's off and I won't be able to vouch for what happens to you sister, understand?"

Kennin nodded and took the envelope.

When Gus González is adopted by a famous TV star,
he expects to be living the good life,
not running for his own.

everyone wants a piece of the rich and famous

Desert Blood
10pm/9c

A NOVEL BY
RONALD CREE

A novel from Simon Pulse
Published by Simon & Schuster